Love, David

Love, David

BY DIANNE CASE
illustrated by Dan Andreasen

LODESTAR BOOKS
Dutton   New York

with love and admiration
for my mother,
a truly remarkable woman

Text copyright © 1986 by Maskew Miller Longman (Pty) Ltd.
Illustrations copyright © 1991 by Dan Andreasen

Library of Congress Cataloging-in-Publication Data
Case, Dianne, 1955–
    Love, David / by Dianne Case; illustrated by Dan Andreasen.—1st American ed.
        p.   cm.
    Summary: Anna recounts the good and bad times with her beloved older brother,
who involves himself in illegal activities to escape from the poverty of his home life
in South Africa.
    ISBN 0-525-67350-4
    [1. Blacks—Fiction. 2. Family problems—Fiction. 3. Brothers and sisters—Fiction.
4. Poor—Fiction. 5. South Africa—Fiction.] I. Andreasen, Dan, ill.   II. Title.
PZ7.C26718Lo   1991
[Fic]—dc20   91-12454
                                                                            CIP
                                                                            AC

First published in the United States in 1991 by Lodestar Books, an affiliate of Dutton
Children's Books, a division of Penguin Books USA Inc., 375 Hudson Street, New
York, New York 10014

Published simultaneously in Canada by McClelland & Stewart, Toronto

Originally published in slightly altered form in South Africa in 1986 by Maskew
Miller Longman Ltd., Howard Drive, Pinelands 7405, P.O. Box 396, Cape Town
8000, South Africa

Printed in the U.S.A.   ISBN: 0-525-67350-4
First American Edition   10 9 8 7 6 5 4 3 2 1

❧ N O T E T O T H E R E A D E R ❧

Love, David is based on a very real section of the South African community. The characters are "colored"—descendants of white farmers or other white settlers and black slaves or indigenous natives in the days before interracial relationships were illegal in this country. The farmers were descendants of the Dutch settlers, and the slaves were imported from Java, Northern Africa, and the East Indies. Their lack of a common language gave rise to the development of the Afrikaans language, which at first was regarded as an inferior form of Dutch.

In the same way that the white Afrikaner was intimidated by the British settlers of South Africa, and tried to speak English in order to be accepted by the British, so the Afrikaans-speaking colored people were intimidated by their English-speaking counterparts, whom they encountered when they migrated to Cape Town. Until very recently, the English language bore some status for those who spoke it.

This story was written with love for my land and my people, with the hope that it will in some way contribute toward reconciliation among the people of this country who for the past forty years, under the apartheid laws, have lived in racially classified groups totally isolated from one another. The book is an attempt to share a culture with those who do not know about it.

Dianne Case
Cape Town, South Africa

Love, David

✺ O N E ✺

The police car sped through the closed hangar-type doors of the paper warehouse. Crash! Wood splintered as the car veered into a neatly stacked pile of paper separated by sheets of cardboard.

In the pandemonium the policeman emerged from the debris—bewildered and covered with strewn sheets of paper. It was just his luck that the thugs made their getaway in his vehicle! Shouting curses, the potbellied policeman ran ridiculously after the police car until it disappeared into the distance.

I let out a snigger and then roared in absolute delight.

I was aware of David's "Shhh!" and then, "Split, guys! Split!" from Oupa.

When I managed to stop laughing, the owner of the house, through whose windows we had been watching TV, was only a few paces from us, waving a broomstick. I jumped from David's back in fright, grazing my knees. David grabbed my hand, hauling me to my feet. He ran so fast that my feet hardly touched the ground until we lost sight of the house.

We are always running—running through the tall grass, running because we are being chased, running to reach some place in the shortest time, to lengthen our day, or running to escape the harshness of the elements. In summer we run to keep the sting of the burning sand from our feet; in winter we run so that the blood in our feet will circulate more quickly, to warm our bodies.

David always says, "If your feet are warm, the rest of your body will be warm, but if your feet are cold, your body will remain cold."

I believe everything that David says. He always seems to know so much. David is my brother, but not in the same way that my sister is my sister. Dadda says that David is my half brother and I am his half sister; Mamsie says that his own father died long ago and that Dadda is his new father. "He still has to get used to him," she says. David says: "I was here before you and him."

That much is true, I know. David has been here as far back as I can remember. Sometimes I think Dadda does not like David. He says David smokes and steals. "That's why he is so small and stupid," he says.

David is small for his fourteen years, but I don't think he's stupid.

One night Dadda found David smoking. He could not escape—he was caught red-handed. Dadda grabbed him by the scruff of his neck and took him around to the back of the fowl *hokkie*—the pen for the chickens. I silently watched from the corner as Dadda beat him with his fist, hurling insults at him all the while. David said nothing and did nothing. His nose and mouth were bleeding. I could see him struggling not to cry. I could not understand why Dadda would not look at David's eyes, which glared cynically at him all the time. Poor David—I don't know where he slept that night.

David does not speak much to our parents. He just says "Yes" to whatever they say to him. Mamsie herself does not say much to David. She only says things like: "Here is your food; go to the shop for a sliced white bread; ask next door for an onion, say I'll give it back; pick the baby up," and things like that. But David is very popular with his friends and with me. I love him very much.

He has two best friends, although he prefers one of them.

He has never said so, but I know. The three of them call themselves the Good Buddies. David is called Buddy D; his friend Johan, fatter, taller, but younger than him, is called Buddy J; the other one, Ashraf, older than David, is called Oupa—sometimes Buddy O, but mostly Oupa. In fact, everyone calls him Oupa. This is because Oupa's legs are malformed, making him walk like a very old man, and *Oupa* means grandfather.

My name is Anna, although no one uses it. Everyone calls me "Meisie"—Mamsie, Dadda, David, his friends, and all the people who know me. That is because I am my father's firstborn daughter, and the word *meisie* means girl in Afrikaans.

The three of them roam about together. They sing, tell jokes, and even make their own music. David has a guitar that he made himself. Oupa plays "drums" on upturned pots and pans or empty paint tins. Oupa has an unusual, high-pitched voice. It is a real treat to hear him sing. He would like to be a professional entertainer one day—like a cousin he talks about admiringly. We all live in a place called "Die Kamp," which is a vast stretch of undeveloped land on which people set up makeshift homes from scraps of wood and iron. These houses are often referred to as shanties or *pondokkies*.

When we want to get away from the Kamp, we often walk to the *vlei*. David carries Baby (she's our baby sister) on his back and I walk alongside him. Buddy J will blow the mouth organ, Oupa will sing in his high-pitched voice, and David will accompany them with humming or whistling. No one speaks. Conversation would spoil the good atmosphere.

David always makes sure that Oupa has a sturdy stick, which he uses for balancing when we go on long walks. He will automatically hand Oupa a "walking stick," which he easily accepts.

3

We also like to watch TV, although this is a risky business. The snag is that we peep through someone's window, naturally in the richer area opposite the *vlei*. We first check that a curtain is slightly open, so that we can see the little screen, then that there are no dogs that will bark and rouse the occupants of the house. We were once surprised and had a bucket of water thrown over us. Often we just manage to escape a beating, like the time we were watching the police comedy.

Breathlessly, we flung ourselves down on the grass. My temples were throbbing and David's chest was heaving from the exhausting run. Buddy J came panting toward us. "What about Oupa?" he cried.

"He'll be all right," David replied. "Everyone feels sorry for him."

❧ T W O ❧

Dadda is a gardener. He is the best that I know of. He grows the most luscious tomatoes and the most beautiful flowers. He also cultivates plants for sale. On a hot day it is very refreshing to cut a ripe tomato through and eat it with salt; or in very cold weather, cooked up with bones, the tomatoes make a delicious tomato *bredie*—a thick stew that is good enough to satisfy the most hungry appetite.

Dadda has worked in many rich people's gardens. Sometimes he comes home and says that he has had a quarrel with whoever he was working for and that he is not going back to them. However, after a few weeks they come and fetch him—that's how good he is. Sometimes, especially over weekends, different people fetch him for a day, sometimes two days. Mamsie does not like him to work for some of these weekend people because she says it does not pay. Many people don't give him money—instead, they give him a bottle of wine. I don't see anything wrong with that because Dadda likes wine, and in any case, Mamsie always complains that he spends too much money on wine.

I know the secret behind Dadda's gardening success. He keeps an old drum filled with water, into which he throws all the vegetable peels, eggshells, and old bones. He nourishes his plants once a week with this revolting-smelling liquid. He also sprinkles the fowls' manure around his plants. Although the drum is covered with a sheet of iron, it is a breeding place for scores of mosquitoes. I hate mosquitoes, especially in summer, when they're a terrible nuisance. In the dead of night when you're dreaming at your best, you'll vaguely notice their buzzing. By then, they'll have bitten you already, leaving nasty, itching bumps all over your arms and legs. It is pitiful when they attack Baby because she becomes irritable and restless. She whines and rubs her eyes and face, clumsily smearing tears, snot, and spit all over her face and arms. I then have to sit and rock her all day. When she and I are alone, I scratch her bites for her as I know this offers some relief from the itching. She sits perfectly still. When these bites draw water, I usually squeeze them so that they will heal quicker. This takes a few days, but by then there will be fresh bites. Mosquitoes are an ongoing problem throughout summer.

One evening Dadda caught me squeezing Baby's bites. He shouted some unrepeatable things at me and gave me a clout over the ear. It was my own fault.

Sometimes David sells some of Dadda's plants—mostly in the wet winter months when the seedlings are ready for transplanting and when we are always terribly hungry.

"Isn't that stealing?" I often ask him.

"It isn't stealing," he replies nonchalantly. "We're only taking—taking what belongs to us too." I shrug my shoulders because I really don't know.

David arranges these seedlings in damp newspaper packages with the roots covered and the leaves showing—just like Dadda does it. We walk up to the traffic light at the crossroads on Prince George Drive. I sit on the pavement while David offers his packages to motorists who stop at the red light. He charges fifty cents and tells the people that it is a bargain. He also tells the people how to plant the seedlings so that they will thrive. At fifty cents it probably is a bargain because some people take three or four packets at a time, and soon he has sold the whole lot.

We then walk past the rich people's houses and go to the shop on the other side of the road. It is bigger than the local café and stocks everything from fruit and chocolates to toys and toothbrushes in a colorful display.

David says it is safer to go to this shop rather than the one nearer to our home when we "do a move." You see, if we spend a lot of money at our local shop, the shopkeeper becomes suspicious, and he may tell Dadda—then there will be trouble. He buys us chips and fizzy cool drinks in tins and bubble gum and a few loose cigarettes for himself. I love bubble gum because you can blow huge, smacking bubbles that spread over your nose and chin when they collapse, sometimes sticking in your hair too. Chewing gum, on the other hand, is a waste of time and money. Try as you may, it never gives a big bubble, breaking open as soon as it should start swelling.

David cups his hand and holds a cigarette between his thumb and forefinger, at the filter. He puffs on it all the way to the *vlei,* where we eat what we have bought and where he has another cigarette. During the winter months there are not many people at the *vlei*—in fact, it is almost always deserted then.

I have many grouses about winter weather. The days are too short, and everything seems dark and damp, even if it is not wet. The cold burns your feet and seems to bite its way into your bones. The house is also cold, damp, and dark. Wet nappies and washing hang over just about everything, and don't you dare touch anything with grubby hands—even by accident!

David must be the worst off during this kind of weather, although he has never said so. He sleeps on cardboard and newspaper on the floor, covered by two thin gray blankets, which he folds in two for maximum warmth. I sleep at the foot end of the bed, at our parents' feet. Baby sleeps at the top with them and gets a chance to sleep on the pillow when she is in the middle.

Mamsie brings the cardboard and newspaper from work. She also works for rich people in Hout Bay. It is very far— it takes two buses from our house. Her madam is a very

7

good person. She always sends us food and cake that they did not finish, clothes that their children have outgrown, and chipped crockery and ornaments. Mamsie always dreams of having a house that is big enough for her to have a display cabinet that she can put all her ornaments in. At the moment they are wrapped in newspaper and placed in a cardboard box under the bed. Dadda does not seem to like Mamsie's madam. Mamsie can beg him for a bunch of flowers to take her, but he will not give in.

"I don't give my flowers away," he insists. "She can have flowers if she pays for them."

"She's good to us," Mamsie argues.

Dadda will give her one of those looks that warns her she had better be quiet—or else. She keeps quiet and then one day when he is not looking she takes some of his seedlings or flowers or both and takes them to work for her madam.

As long as I can remember, Mamsie has worked for the same madam, or family, as she sometimes says. The only time that she was home was the week that Baby was born. That was when David stopped going to school. He had to stay home to look after Baby. He washed her nappies, bathed her, prepared her bottles, and took her to the clinic for her injections.

Everything was working out fine until David's teacher came to find out why he was not going to school anymore. Dadda said he would have to go back to school or Dadda and Mamsie would get into trouble.

Since then, I have been looking after Baby, but I don't know what will happen when I go to school one day.

As it is, I should have been going to school already for several years. Mamsie had to take time off work to book me in, but she kept forgetting. By the time she went to the school—David's school—there was no more room for me. The principal said we should try another school, but Mamsie said we must wait. Dadda was very cross, but what could he do? When Mamsie asked him if he was going to take me to the other school, which was much farther, he did not answer her. He only mumbled about the terrible things he was going to do to David's principal.

David laughed because he didn't like his principal. I was terribly disappointed because I want to be clever when I'm big. Mind you, with David's help, I can write my name and I recognize many words. I am also very good at adding money.

⚓ T H R E E ⚓

Mamsie and Dadda speak Afrikaans to each other, to the neighbors, and to David, but they speak English to me and Baby. When I ask them about this strange habit, all I hear is "We want you to be better" from both of them. What's in a language?

Dadda comes from a place up-country, near to Swellendam, called Elim. He says it is a quiet, beautiful, peaceful little village. He has not seen his family, who he reckons still lives there, for many years. I would like to meet them, just to know who my cousins, aunts, and uncles are. Dadda says we'll go there one day—"When we have our own car, we'll go there every weekend!"

David laughs at the idea. "Forget it," he says. "He is all talk—just talk!"

I don't know.

"There isn't enough work there for everyone," Dadda says.

Mamsie's family used to live at a place called Cook's Bush, which was close to where we are now. Oupa's family also comes from the Bush. When everyone had to leave the Bush to make way for new houses that were being built there, Mamsie's family was scattered. She has four sisters and three brothers but does not know where they are. She seems to have an idea that her second eldest sister has a sleep-in job in Hout Bay somewhere but says that if she saw her, she might not recognize her. She thinks that her youngest brother could be dead, as he had rheumatic fever when they left the Bush. Otherwise, she is in the dark.

I feel very sad when I think about Mamsie's life. She

11

does not seem to get much pleasure from it. Life for her is one ongoing slog. She is always tired and her legs have dark blue veins that stick out all over them. They look like swollen bruises except that they are in squiggly lines.

I did not know what they were until David told me, adding that we all have veins.

"Ours don't look like that," I argued.

"That's because we are still young," David replied.

"I hope mine never get like that," I said thoughtfully.

"They probably will," David teased.

Besides her blue veins, Mamsie's feet are always swollen when she gets home at night. Her working day is very long. She has to leave home when it is still dark to wake up her madam's family at seven o'clock. By that time she will have prepared their breakfast and laid out their clothes. Her day ends after she has washed the supper dishes and tidied the kitchen. By the time she gets home most nights, it is already dark.

One thing about her, though, is that she must enjoy her job, since she is loyal no matter what the circumstances are. She will not miss a day at work, not even during the colder months when she suffers severely from flu. Since the riots, most of the buses have no windows, making her catch more colds. She is always coughing, sniffling, and sneezing. She comes home shivering and complaining about "those children who don't want to learn and spend their time throwing stones at buses."

"You've been listening to too much of your merrem's talk again," Dadda says irritably, blaming Mamsie's madam. "The *skollies* have done that to the buses," Dadda argues. "You think your merrem knows everything."

"You can't blame the bus people for not replacing the windows," Mamsie says to cool Dadda's anger.

"They make enough money," Dadda retorts. "All they

do is put up the fares, every time—put up the fares. Where is all that money going to?''

"Merrem says it's the price of petrol that is so dear," Mamsie says in an effort to steer the conversation in another direction.

"Change your job and do yourself a favor," Dadda says aggressively. "Who does your merrem think she is, living in luxury, but you must wash her underwear?"

"Ag, man, you know she pays me for that and I can't leave those children. They are like my own. I made them big!" she says with pride. "I heard their first words and watched their first steps. How can I leave them? And they are very good to me!"

"Yes," Dadda says, "they are good to you. They give you a hundred rand a month and they are good to you!"

"Who else will give me that?" Mamsie insists.

"It's no use talking to you," Dadda says, taking a swig from his bottle. "No brains—that's your problem."

Mamsie's madam is very fond of her. She lets her sleep at their house during the bus boycotts and riots. She says it is safer than her coming in with all the trouble on the roads. Mind you, she often sleeps over at their house when they entertain and through the December holidays, when they have visitors from up-country.

I often panic when I consider Mamsie's life. Where will it end, will the pattern ever change? Sometimes I feel stuck, as if we are all trapped in a spinning circle and as if the pattern of our lives is already planned. I become very sad when I realize how closely my life could follow my mother's life-pattern.

One day I was thinking about my future when I realized that we all have choices. We can decide, in our own lives, the path each of us will follow. These choices make us the person we will be. Although Mamsie's choices were all good, to the benefit of others, they were bad for her own life.

This idea came to me a long time ago. We were playing at the *vlei,* imitating some characters in a television series. Oupa was sitting in a bluegum tree, which was the "helicopter." David and Buddy J had to run and jump into this "chopper," which Oupa was "flying" low enough for them to reach. They ran, grabbed a low-lying branch, and hoisted themselves up into the tree. It was impossible for me to grab at even the twigs, since this branch was definitely out of my reach. I sat down under the tree and was about to throw a tantrum. That was when I realized that I had a choice. I could scream and demand that David lift me up into the tree, or I could ignore the challenge and wait for them to come down, when I would join the game again. I had a choice, and this made me the person that I was growing up to be. If I threw a tantrum, I would be miserable and a nuisance to David and his friends. If I didn't, I would be a pleasant playmate, someone nice to have around. I also had a choice in sulking or not sulking. The choice was my very own. The choice was me.

This sense of awakening made me ecstatic. I was in control of my life and the person that I wanted to be.

I am me.

✦ F O U R ✦

Very early one Sunday morning David, Oupa, Buddy J, and I were sitting at the *vlei* trying to catch some trout—a freshwater fish found in the *vlei*. Once before, we had seen a group of fishermen hauling the largest trout out of the *vlei*. We had already tried so many times that we decided to be here as early as possible. "Before the traffic upsets the fish," as Oupa reasoned.

Oupa had brought along a reel of gut, which David and Buddy J had cut into three lengths and fastened to three sticks. They tied on a squiggly, squirmy, multicolored, hairy worm to the free end of the gut. About a centimeter or two higher than the bait, each securely tied a stone.

They cast their lines into the water and impatiently waited, pulled them up, secured fresh bait (because the other bait had vanished), and perhaps better sinkers too; but no fish bit at the lines.

We sat for a while listening to David's and Oupa's jokes. Oupa is a real clown. Sometimes his jokes had no humor, but his expressions and voice imitations still had us in stitches. We would roll and laugh until our sides ached.

"Van der Merwe was visiting an American," he began. "The American said, 'My farm is so big, if I get in my car and drive all day, I can't reach the other end.' Van der Merwe said: 'Yes, I also had a car like that once.' "

Buddy J laughed so much that his fat stomach wobbled. This made us laugh more. "Shh," Oupa said.

A beautiful, shiny, powder-blue car stopped near us. The driver sat in the car and looked around carefully.

"He's up to something," Oupa said.

"Let's hide and watch him," David suggested.

"Good idea!" Buddy J exclaimed.

They left their lines on the ground, and with very little noise or movement, we backed into the bushes, safely out of sight. The driver got out of his car and opened the trunk, lifting out a black rubbish bag. He gathered some biggish stones and rocks and put these into the bag, all the time looking suspiciously around him. He rushed back to the car and dropped what looked like a dirty, white, fluffy ball into the bag as well and quickly tied the bag with a piece of wire.

"I think it's a white teddy bear," I whispered to David, crouching next to me.

"Shh!" he replied, placing his right forefinger over his lips.

The man was now hurriedly dragging the heavy bag toward the water, all the while looking warily about him. He picked up one of our sticks and prodded the bag until it sank down into the water.

Blimp! Blimp! Blimp!

The bag disappeared.

After watching for a while, the man turned on his heel, wiping his hands on his faded blue denim jeans. He jumped into the car and sped away, leaving a cloud of dust behind him.

"I think it's a kitten," Buddy J said thoughtfully. "Some people don't keep queen cats."

David removed his sweater and trousers and dived into the water.

"People can be so cruel," Oupa said, as if to himself.

David surfaced and called to Buddy J, motioning with his left arm that he should come into the water to help him.

"I can't," Buddy J cried, looking helpless. "There's quicksand there."

"Coward!" Oupa spat at Buddy J.

David was submerged again. Breathlessly, we watched until he surfaced. "Tear the bag open," Oupa shouted to him. "You'll never be able to bring the bag out—it's too heavy."

David tore the bag open. Immediately it began to fill with water, but he managed to rescue the fluffy ball.

"It does look like a cat," Oupa said.

Blimp! The *vlei* devoured the rubbish bag in one gulp.

"It looks dead—I'm sure it's dead," Buddy J remarked as David struggled out of the water.

"It's a puppy," David said exhaustedly, sitting down, dripping wet, on the grass.

He gently placed the still little animal beside him. We watched it, holding our breath.

The pathetic, defenseless creature started shivering. It simply lay there, blinking its soft brown eyes. Entranced, as if expecting a thank-you from it, the three boys sat watching it.

"He must be cold," I said, bringing them all back to earth.

Wordlessly, David offered his sweater to Oupa, who wrapped the puppy in it.

"Rub him dry," David said, clearly claiming ownership.

Oupa rubbed him for a while and then he wriggled free. Oupa picked him up again. "*Siestog,* man!" he exclaimed. "Shame. Look here—he's only got three legs. One of his back legs is missing."

We all looked at the puppy's legs. One of his back legs *was* missing. All you could see was a stump.

"He must have been born like that," David said firmly.

"No wonder they didn't want him," Buddy J said. "What are we going to do with a three-legged dog?"

"It's not his fault," David said.

"But people will laugh at us," Buddy J insisted.

"Let them laugh," Oupa said sternly.

"Yes," David added. "It's not his fault."

That was the day that Stumpy came into our lives.

❧ F I V E ☙

Dadda does not like dogs and cats, and David knows that. But he took Stumpy home anyway. He placed a cardboard box in his corner and put the dog in it. The poor thing sat in the box all day. He did not move or make a sound. David bought half a liter of milk and, having warmed it, spent the rest of the afternoon spoon-feeding the dog with a teaspoon. Mamsie was becoming anxious as the evening wore on.

"You know the place is small," she said. "He'll be home any minute now."

David did not hear her or pretended not to hear.

"Your father is going to be mad," she continued.

David still said nothing. He was clearly besotted with the sad little puppy.

Our house is terribly small. In fact, it is no more than one room, which Dadda built himself. He always speaks of extending it one day. "When I have enough money," he says, adding, "even secondhand poles and zincs are expensive." Anyhow, we have managed with the one room for as long as I can remember. The bed is in the middle of the room. All our extra clothes, pots, and valuable things, such as our ornaments, are stored in cardboard boxes under the bed. A corner under the bed on Dadda's side is reserved for the chamber pot. We all know to keep that corner free for it. Behind the door is a hook on which our everyday clothes and towel hang. The front section of the room is used as a kitchen. There is a wooden table and a chair, which are scrubbed every Friday. (This is my job, but David sometimes does it for me rather than watch me do it.)

Dadda made the table himself and Mamsie brought the chair from work. The legs of the chair were broken, but Dadda soon fixed that. On the table, in the corner, is a bucket of water. This is our drinking water. It is David's duty to make sure that the bucket is always filled. On the other corner of the table stands our Primus stove. I was warned that I must never, but *never,* attempt to use this. There would surely be a disaster and I would die a terrible death. So I never try to use that stove.

The kitchen area is separated from the sleeping area by a tatty, faded curtain which has always hung there, so I don't know where it came from. Above the table are wooden shelves that Dadda built and which Mamsie decorated with newspaper. She cut it into pretty patterns, leaving the edges zigzagged to look like doilies. This is tacked down and is changed once in a while. Our few cups and plates are packed on these shelves. Our plastic basin, used for washing the dishes, as well as our galvanized iron bath, are kept underneath the table.

Bathing is quite an occasion in our house. Every Saturday evening Dadda boils water in a paraffin tin on an open fire in the yard. He then comes in and fills the bath with hot water and he bathes first. Mamsie bathes next, but sometimes skips because she bathes at work when her madam is out. Next, Baby and I bathe together. David bathes last. Mamsie then soaks the week's washing in the same water. The following morning David and Dadda carry the bath outside and Mamsie does the washing then.

During summer our house is uncomfortably stuffy and hot, but just bearable. In winter it is icy cold and damp, and we feel closed in because of the wet washing everywhere. Everyone is irritable and short-tempered.

When it rains, you'd swear that the tin roof is going to fall in at any moment as the rain beats down heavily on it. Sometimes the roof leaks, but Dadda soon fixes that. The yard gets flooded. Everyone puts logs and rocks in the water and we have to jump from one to the other so as not to get wet. Sometimes we just walk through the water, but this can be dangerous if there are broken bottles and other sharp things that can cut our feet. During April and May, when a ghostly wind howls, I lie awake all night. Dadda too tosses and turns. I have to be careful that he does not kick me in his sleep or I'll fall off the bed.

Buddy J says that it is a good thing that our house is so small because if you have a bigger house, like theirs, people keep on bothering you to rent a part of it to them.

For the first few days that Stumpy was with us, David placed the dog's box under the bed at the foot end, near his own head. Very, very early the next morning, he'd remove it so that Dadda knew nothing about it. Dadda slept like a log when he had a drink, but Mamsie's nerves were raw.

One night, Dadda came home sober. During the night Stumpy sometimes used to whimper in his sleep. He probably had nightmares. Well, this particular night Dadda sat up immediately. He strained his ears, jumped out of bed in the dark, and noisily pulled everything out from under the bed, upsetting the chamber pot in the process. (This we discovered the following day.) I cringed as I waited for Stumpy to be found. No one dared stir or murmur when Dadda's anger was roused. Shouting and swearing, he flung the box with Stumpy out into the dark night. He banged the door behind him. I peered down at David's unmoving figure. An icy chill went through me as I saw the fierce hatred glaring from my brother's eyes.

❧ S I X ❧

The following evening, after a long day of worrying, I decided to talk to Dadda about keeping Stumpy.

"He's infested with fleas," Dadda said calmly. "That's why he cries in his sleep and that's why we can't keep him."

"But what will happen to him?" I pleaded.

"The SPCA will have to find a home for him," he answered sharply—so closing the subject.

Meanwhile, Oupa said that he would keep the dog at his house, but every morning, as soon as we opened our door, there Stumpy would be, sitting on the step waiting for us. He would yap and jump about excitedly when he saw David, who would pick him up and take him for a walk.

David had to be careful about Stumpy so as not to anger Dadda, who must have decided to turn a blind eye to him. Mamsie told us to make sure that Stumpy never came into the house because Dadda would blow his top.

"It seems we can keep him," I confided to David.

"He *is* full of fleas," David replied thoughtfully.

Every afternoon for a full week, David and I would sit catching Stumpy's fleas. He would remove them from the wiggling Stumpy's stomach, one by one. It was easy to spot the black fleas in Stumpy's white fur. David would roll the flea between his right forefinger and his thumb and then place it in the jar lid that I held. I would crush it under my nail, spattering the blood that it had sucked from poor Stumpy.

"It's no use," David said when I appeared one morning with the lid of the jar. "We need some flea powder."

23

"Buy some, then," I said.

"I don't have any money," he replied, "but I'll make a plan."

David looked for an empty plastic bottle, which he filled with water. He took two of Baby's nappies from the line and later on, we all took a walk to the traffic light at Prince George Drive. Stumpy, Baby, and I sat on the pavement while David washed the windows of motorists returning from work.

Some of the motorists gave him a few coins, some gave him their sandwiches that they had not eaten that day, while others crossly shooed him away from their cars. He put the money in his pocket and handed me the sandwiches after a quick look at their contents. If he silently gave me a sandwich, it meant that I could have it. If he wanted one for himself, he'd say, "That's mine." I would keep that particular one aside for him.

When the traffic lessened, David decided that we could go home. But first he sat on the pavement and counted his money, beaming at his success.

The following morning, David skipped school and took a bus to Wynberg. He returned a few hours later with a tin of flea powder and a leather collar for Stumpy, as well as a lip-smacking parcel of fish and chips, which he had bought at a fish shop near the bus terminal.

✌ S E V E N ❧

A blue minibus comes to the clearing near the Kamp on Sunday afternoons. The occupants—"brothers and sisters" who call themselves the Wayside Seekers—tell us Bible stories and teach us choruses under the tall bluegum trees. After the services we are all given a few delicious sweets. Many children come to the services—even the Muslim children. Some of the adults attend but stand shyly in the distance until one of the "brothers" or "sisters" calls them to join in.

The Wayside Sunday School is the highlight of the week for some children, who dress for the occasion; others, like myself, come only for the sweets. This particular Sunday the story was about David and Goliath. When the hero's name was mentioned, everyone looked at David, who pretended not to notice.

After the service, David took a pair of Mamsie's panty hose from the line and made a sling out of them, and we all took a walk to the *vlei* to try it out. I had to carry Baby, who was growing very heavy and naughty. She would cry for everything and everyone spoiled her. David bought her a lollipop every afternoon when he came from school. I tried to teach her to be good and smacked her little hands when we were alone in the mornings.

Stumpy had also grown big. He was a cheeky, heavy, round ball and barked at everything and everyone. He was a hero among the other dogs, who were always following him around the Kamp.

We each had a chance to try the sling. We swung it round

and round and flung it into the air. David and Oupa threw the farthest and Buddy J was not bad—but mine!

"Smell that *braai!*" Oupa said.

"Yes," David replied. "It makes you hungry."

Many people come to *braai* at the *vlei* on Sunday afternoons. When they leave, we hunt through whatever they left behind. Sometimes, when we are lucky, we find a whole breadroll with a piece of sausage in it that some child has wasted, or perhaps a chop that has fallen in the sand and has been left. We often find the remains of a chop from which only the middle piece has been eaten, and watermelon peels that still have lots of red flesh left.

"Rich people are so wasteful," I said to Buddy J. "Mamsie often says so."

David and Oupa collected cigarette ends that they could still smoke.

Dusk was falling and all the visitors had left except a group of older teenagers, who were sitting on swings. "The faster you swing the sling, the farther it will fall," Oupa said to David.

David swung the sling around and around until it whistled and then he hurled it through the air. The stone hit one of the teenagers before landing next to the swing. David rushed over to apologize and to get the sling back. Before he could say a word, the older boy ran up to him and smacked his face so hard that his nose began to bleed. Through tear-filled eyes, David glared at him, while taking a few steps backward. Like lightning, he darted forward and knocked the lanky boy to the ground. He jumped on him and, in a fit of temper, smacked him in the face with his right hand, with his left hand, with his right hand, with his left, spilling the blood from his bleeding nose all over the boy.

Thwak! Thwak! Thwak! Thwak! Thwak!

I started crying as I saw the others approach and haul David off their friend. Baby, perched on my hip, was crying too. All at once, Oupa appeared, waving his stick through the air.

"Comrades!" he shouted. "Comrades—make peace, brothers!"

The other boys looked at one another and at Oupa. They slowly released David. They hit one another's hands to show comradeship. David reluctantly did the same, but I saw a look of revenge in his eyes. He was not done with them yet! He silently took my hand and we walked off to the tap together, leaving Oupa and Buddy J talking to their new-found "comrades."

David pulled off his shirt and washed the blood out of it. He washed his face and also mine and Baby's. Oupa and Buddy J were approaching.

"Oupa knows them!" Buddy J shouted excitedly.

"The one's brother used to work with my cousin," Oupa explained.

David was not impressed and showed no reaction. Besides, he does not believe anything Oupa says. Oupa had once told us the story of the *vlei*'s name.

"You must never swim in the *vlei*," he had said authoritatively. "It is haunted."

He had pointed to a beautiful white water lily in full bloom. "Do you see that?" he asked. "That is the spirit of a princess who lived many years ago. She used to come to the *vlei* to swim. One day she saw a beautiful water lily and reached out to pick it. The lily seemed to wade out of her reach, but she wanted it, so she waded out after it, slowly reaching the middle of the *vlei;* then she and the water lily suddenly vanished. She was never seen again but comes back every year as a water lily to lure people into the *vlei*."

27

That story really upset me, but when I told David about it, he said that I mustn't believe everything that Oupa said.

"You can thank your lucky stars that Oupa knew the Comrades, Buddy D," Buddy J was saying, hopping alongside us.

"Ag, shut up," David said.

✍ E I G H T ☙

Autumn arrived, with its cool air, southeasterly winds, and dry, colored leaves rustling down to form a crunchy carpet under our feet. The mornings were a bit cold, but as soon as the sun appeared, it was still lovely and warm. I spent the mornings sitting in the sun while Baby crawled about in the yard looking for water to mess in.

Two hens were broody and sitting on eggs. The rooster was such a bully that he used to gobble up all the mealies and the hens had no chance of having a decent feed.

"I shall have to slaughter him," Dadda muttered to himself. "In any case, there are bound to be some roosters hatching soon."

Dadda stayed home from work one morning and caught the rooster. (I think he had had another fight with his latest boss.) The rooster kicked and squawked, but Dadda held him securely at the base of his wings. He took the rooster, who now was surely shouting "Murder!" in his language, to the back of the house so the other fowls did not have to see him kill their mate—bully though he was.

Dadda held the rooster between his legs and, with one quick movement of his hand, broke his neck. He put the now limp bird down on the dry grass. The bird gave a few jerky kicks and then lay dead still, his eyes quickly losing their focus and life. Blood trickled from his mouth. He was well and truly dead now. Dadda took his chopper and chopped the head right off.

By this time, a number of children had gathered round us and were excitedly watching Dadda's every move.

"Get away from here!" he shouted at them irritably.

At once they jumped out of his way, moving back into the distance, but slowly, one by one, came nearer and nearer until Dadda shouted at them again. This continued for as long as we were sitting there.

Dadda placed the rooster in our washing-up basin and poured boiling water on him. He took a spade and covered the blood with dry sand so that no flies would sit on it. Afterward Dadda and I sat and pulled the bird's feathers out. This was a job that I enjoyed very much, and I was proud that he let me help. Every time Dadda stood up to fetch more boiling water, the little onlookers would scurry out of his way, but he took no notice of them.

The bird looked so funny with all his feathers removed, so naked. His flesh was a pinky color. Dadda inserted his hand into the body and removed all the innards. The bird's crop was still full of whole mealies.

Dadda made a hole and buried the water with the feathers and entrails. He hung the rooster up by the legs until he had prepared the pot for cooking him.

That night, when Mamsie came from work, supper was ready—roast chicken and lots of roast potatoes. One thing about Dadda—when he cooks, he makes a lot of food. I had three roast potatoes. Everyone enjoyed the meat— everyone that is, except David, who refused to eat it.

"He must stay hungry," Dadda said, licking his fingers. "There is nothing else to eat."

"Eat it," I urged David.

"I don't want any," he said.

"Look at that," Mamsie said, pointing to Baby.

"Siestog," Dadda said and bent to kiss her on her cheek.

Baby was absorbed in the pleasure of sucking the drumstick, oil and spit running down her arms. She growled like a puppy when Dadda kissed her.

"Leave her alone," Mamsie said. "She's busy."

❧ N I N E ❧

It was school holidays, and lately David had been going out on his own. Whenever I wanted to go with him, he'd say: "You stay at home. I won't be long. You'll see; I'll be back now-now. Maybe I'll bring you something."

Sometimes David would be away for hours, returning when it was nighttime and we were all in bed. At times Mamsie would stay up, perhaps ironing or preparing the following night's supper. She would look through the window from time to time but would not say anything to Dadda.

"Where were you?" she'd ask David when he eventually arrived.

Of course, he would not answer her. He would hurriedly lay his blankets out and get undressed without eating the supper that Mamsie had kept for him. "You smell like fire," Mamsie would say in an effort to make conversation with him, but he would lie still with his eyes closed. I could not understand him. "There is going to be trouble when your father notices," Mamsie would continue. "Then he and I are going to have terrible words over you, David!"

During the day, when I anxiously waited for David, I would play on the field behind our house. I felt so alone those times. I would lie in the grass and pick up all the little insects that I could find and put them in an empty coffee tin. Sometimes I found chameleons and let them walk on me. Buddy J was terrified of chameleons. If he saw one, he'd run like mad. I loved watching the chameleons catching insects with their long tongues, which they would unroll in an instant.

When there was a little breeze blowing, I would lie flat

on my back and watch the clouds. They reminded me of people. I could see a mother with her children. She was in a great hurry. Every so often she would turn around and count her children; then she would hurry on again, pause again to count them, and then hurry on once more until she would be absorbed, along with her children, into another huge cloud. There were many women clouds. Every so often they would pause for a little chat. As soon as their menfolk appeared, they would hurry on by, as if they had not stopped at all, not even to greet one another. They, too, would eventually unite with the larger group of clouds.

At times an airplane would come past. I would close my eyes and lie perfectly still. It would be war. The enemy was approaching. I jumped up and grabbed a stick. That was my gun. Carefully, I moved through the tall, dry grass until they could no longer see me.

Bang! Bang! Bang! I shot the enemy out of the sky.

Buddy J told me that he would like to be a pilot one day. He said he would pilot a huge jet and come flying over the Kamp. He would wave to all of us and maybe, if his boss allowed, he would give us all a ride in his jet.

"That's stupid," Oupa said. "You can't see people from up there. Maybe you'll see the Kamp, but definitely not the people."

"I will have a special windshield," Buddy J said seriously. David and Oupa gave each other one of their special glances that meant that Buddy J was being ridiculous again.

"I want to be a madam one day," I said. "I'll have a real house with electric lights and a bathroom and running water in the house and a beautiful garden outside. Maybe one of you can work for me in my garden."

"If I don't become an entertainer," Oupa said, "I'd like to be an artist and paint pictures of the countryside."

"You could do that well," Buddy J replied. "Look at the beautiful things you draw with a plain pencil."

"What about you, Buddy D?" Oupa asked David.

"I don't know," David said. "I've never thought about it. As long as I'm not poor, I don't mind what I am."

"He wants to be a main man," Buddy J joked.

"I want to be rich," David said to no one in particular, "and drive a fancy, fast car."

David and Oupa sometimes treated Buddy J like an outsider. David only just put up with him. Anyway, his parents owned the house whose yard our house was built in. I have heard that we at first lived in their house with them. That was when I was a little baby. There was always trouble, as happens when a lot of families share the same home. Everyone is bound to get in everyone else's way. There are still many families staying in their house with them, but then it's big and can take them all, although there is always a quarrel of some sort under way.

Dadda is a funny person. He takes his drink, but he does not worry anybody. He could not stand the trouble over small things that he was involved in every day. That is why he built our house away from the rest of them. Because of Dadda's unsociable ways, no one from the big house comes to visit him and he does not visit any of them either. He does not even bother to greet them. Dadda does not like us to play with the other children either.

"As long as we pay our rent, we owe them nothing," he always tells Mamsie.

The adults can sometimes be so petty.

Before Baby was born, Katrien, one of the women from the big house, offered to look after her when she arrived and Mamsie went back to work. When the time came, she first wanted to know how much Mamsie was going to pay her. When Mamsie told her, she was very dissatisfied.

"Then don't worry," Mamsie said. "I'll make some other arrangements."

"I'll just be working for bus fare and Katrien," Mamsie

told Dadda later on. "I won't have enough money left to buy the child's milk. I'll have to keep David home for a while. He will have to look after the baby until we can make other arrangements."

"Katrien's mad!" Dadda said. "She's too lazy to go out to look for work!"

Katrien was furious, as she had wanted the money.

Mamsie sometimes hung the nappies on the shared clothesline before she went to work. That was very early because of the time she had to catch a bus. Later on, when we all got up, the nappies would be lying in the mud. It made me very angry, and I knew that it was Katrien. I would then have to pick the nappies up. I told Mamsie about it, but she said not to worry about it and that she would speak to Katrien. She asked me not to tell Dadda anything about it, but one day when he did not go to work, he found out firsthand. He was fuming and said some ugly things to Katrien. In a rage, he took Baby and me with him on a bus to Wynberg, where he bought some wire to make our own lines. It is a special type of line because the washing does not rust in the wet winter months. Now everyone wants to use our lines. Mamsie does not mind, but she tells all the neighbors to see that their washing is off the lines by the time that Dadda comes home.

"You know what kind of person he is," she says.

If Dadda knew about that, there would be a lot of unpleasantness, but I won't tell him anything. In any case, Mamsie asked me not to.

"It is not nice to be a troublemaker," she said.

✤ T E N ✤

This winter was cold and wet. I do not remember a harsher one. "I forgot that it could be so cold," I told David, rubbing my arms. It had stormed for nearly two weeks. Everything was wet, wet, wet.

Outside, the water was standing like a dam between the houses. Some houses were flooded knee-deep with water. We were lucky that Dadda had built our floor raised.

In such weather Dadda cannot work. He was very moody because he had no money. Mamsie was also in a bad mood. When she got home, she would be drenched to her under-clothes. Her raincoat did not stop the rain from wetting her clothes. The house was full of wet washing. There were no dry nappies for Baby, and Dadda was tearing our sheets up for this purpose. He had hung lines inside the house, but the weather was so cold that it took a couple of days before the nappies would dry, and then they would have to be ironed to get the cold out of them.

Baby was hoarse and feverish. Every morning before she left for work, Mamsie would ask Dadda to take Baby to the Day Hospital. That would be her first concern when she returned at night.

"I am not the child's mother!" Dadda would snap at her when she questioned his reason for not taking Baby to the hospital. That made Mamsie even more miserable. I could understand that she was tired because she would have to sit up most of the night with Baby, who was as hot as a fire. "I must be mother and father in this house," Mamsie

36

moaned. "I must go out to earn the money while you lie at home, and you can't even take your own child to the hospital!"

"Watch out, woman!" Dadda would say, puffing himself up. I sat and looked at them with my heart in my throat. If Dadda lost his temper, he would beat Mamsie up, and then she would stay at her work for a few weeks. She had done it before. It was terrible.

Dadda could not help it that he could not work in the rain, but I knew better than to put my mouth into their affairs.

During the morning Dadda would make a big pot of soup. He would spend the rest of the day cleaning the house. He criticized Mamsie's ability to be a housewife all the while.

"I don't know how she manages to keep a job," he muttered. "Look at the dust all over these boxes under the bed." He lay flat on his stomach and pulled all the boxes out from underneath the bed. "Your mother keeps a lot of junk," he said to me. "I'm throwing away all the things that we can't use."

He emptied each box, one at a time, and then repacked it and put it back in its place. He emptied a box full of old shoes and bags that Mamsie had brought from work.

"No one will ever wear this," he said. "Your mother thinks that if that woman gives her anything, she must be eternally grateful. I'm throwing it all away."

Suddenly something caught his eye. His expression changed at once. "What's going on here?" he shouted. "Wait until I get my hands on that boy. He is stone cold dead!"

Just then David walked in. When he saw the things that Dadda had in his hands, he went absolutely pale. He immediately turned on his heel and ran.

"What is it, Dadda?" I asked curiously. It looked like a lot of multicolored wires and steel things to me—nothing I knew.

"Stolen stuff!" Dadda shouted. "The little thief! He's going to sit in jail one day—just like his father!" That was a shock. It was the first time that I had heard anyone speak about David's father. I knew it was not the time to ask questions. Dadda was still fuming when Mamsie came home. She burst out crying when she saw the things.

"What are they?" she cried.

"Stolen car radios," Dadda answered. "The thief! He's clever enough to hide them in an old towel. Wait until I get my hands on him. I'm going to give him a beating that he'll never forget. Look how stupid he is at school, but he's clever enough to do these things!"

"Please," Mamsie begged. "He's already so scared of you. You know he's so puny too."

"I will not have a thief under my roof!" Dadda roared, so that the veins in his neck stood out.

Baby was now sobbing. She gets frightened when Dadda shouts. Mamsie put Baby on my lap and walked out into the cold, wet, windy, dark night—to look for David, I think. She was away a long time. Eventually, Baby and I lay down on the bed. We both fell asleep. Afterward, through a deep sleep, I became aware of familiar voices. I lay still and listened. Then I remembered what had taken place. It was Oupa's voice. I sat up and looked at him. He was examining the stolen things. There was no sign of David.

"I don't know anything about it," Oupa said. "Don't worry, Mrs. Jantjies, I think David will probably come home tomorrow."

"Thanks for coming, Oupa," Mamsie said.

"It's nothing," Oupa said shyly, and left.

Dadda and Mamsie were so cross with each other that

they were not even speaking. The silence was so real, you could almost feel it. At least Dadda had calmed down a bit.

It was probably very late. Cruel rain beat down hard on our tin roof. Thunder roared in the distance and lightning lit up the whole room for a moment.

I thought of David somewhere in the open veld, near the *vlei*, maybe. He would probably look for shelter under the trees, but what shelter did a tree offer on a night like this? What if the *vlei* should flood? He could drown! What about the ghost of the princess?

Where did David get those things anyway? Could he have stolen them? No, I didn't think so. No.

Why did he run away so fast? It was probably the look of anger on Dadda's face. Maybe the police would find him. Maybe they already had. What if they beat him up? Oupa told us of their ruthless ways. What if they killed him? What if he was already dead? I imagined David lying dead somewhere in a cold prison cell, but it was too painful, so I tried not to think about it.

Lightning once again lit up David's corner, showing its emptiness—his blankets were still neatly stacked in a pile. It was too much for me to bear. I silently allowed my warm tears to flow down my cheeks. All at once, I found myself sobbing, the most heartsore that I can remember. Suddenly I felt two strong hands on me.

''Okay, okay,'' Dadda said. ''Come and sleep up here in my arms.''

Dadda explained to me that he loved David as much as we did, but that he was trying to teach him good ways because David was rebellious. He said that he was not as angry with David as he was disappointed in him. He said that David would be all right and that he would return in the morning.

''I'm sure that Oupa is also involved,'' Mamsie said.

❧ E L E V E N ☙

The rain was over. The sun shone beautifully in a sky of the clearest blue, as if it wanted to make up for the previous three weeks. It was still achingly cold. Mamsie said that there was snow on the mountains in Ceres and that the wind was blowing the cold here. Her madam had told her that. It made sense, except that there was no wind. Where was Ceres, anyway?

David had not been home for nearly a week. I went with Dadda to show him all David's haunts, but we did not find him anywhere. Dadda was back at work, and Baby and I were alone again. The yard was muddy and messy, so I could not allow Baby to play in it. I held her on my lap and pretended to be her mother. I sat on the step and held my fore and middle fingers together as if I were smoking. I blew ''smoke'' into the cold air, pretending that I was the madam of the house.

I soon became bored with that game because Baby was so heavy and kept trying to wriggle free so that she could go and play in the mud with the other children. I wished we could go for a walk to the *vlei* but dared not think of going on my own.

Mamsie said that if Baby became feverish I must give her a teaspoon of the green medicine we had. I felt her forehead. It was a little warm. I got up to fetch the medicine and a teaspoon and was thinking of having a teaspoon or two for myself when a sound distracted me. I stopped in my tracks. There it was again. *Pssst! Pssst!*

I looked around. There was nothing. The other children didn't notice anything. Suddenly I heard the familiar yapping. I knew at once that it was Stumpy. David must be nearby.

I ran to the zinc fence and peered through one of the holes. Yes, there were David and Stumpy. Excitedly, I ran around the fence to meet them.

"Who's at home?" David asked anxiously.

"Just Baby and me," I answered.

"Good!" he said and led the way in through the gap in the fence.

Stumpy was so excited that he ran around the house barking and jumping. His tail wagged so fast that his bottom shook from side to side. He jumped on the bed and off again, messing mud on everything. He licked Baby all over her mouth and face, throwing her off balance. David was very aloof.

"And so?" he asked, lifting the lid from the pot.

"Where were you?" I asked him. "Mamsie was very worried about you, and your teacher sent a letter with Buddy J. Whose clothes are those?"

He was not listening to me. He picked Baby up and threw her into the air, catching her as she fell down. She loved that game. She giggled with delight.

"Isn't there anything to eat in the house?" David asked.

"No," I answered. "Mamsie is going to bring us some food tonight."

The next thing, David was lying under the bed scratching in all the things that Dadda had packed so neatly.

"Where is the stuff?" he asked agitatedly.

"Dadda threw it away. Whose was it anyway?"

"It belonged to my *broer*," he said.

"Oupa?" I asked, remembering what Mamsie had said.

"Oupa isn't my *broer*," David said disgustedly. "He's a kid."

"He's older than you, David," I said, defending the absent Oupa.

"He's still a kid," David insisted.

"Look here," he said, rolling up his sleeve.

He showed me the most beautiful watch that I had ever seen.

"It's lovely," I gasped.

"It's a digital," David said proudly. "My *broer* gave it to me."

I was fascinated by the watch, especially the changing numbers. I was particularly tickled by the 8 changing into a 9.

"You may wear it a little," David said, removing it from his arm.

I was suddenly scared that if I wore it, it would take away its beauty.

"Where did he throw it?" David asked, fastening the watch on my wrist. "What did he have to say?"

"He said he loves you, David," I said slowly.

"Don't make me laugh," David said, with sarcasm in his voice. "He talks any crap to you. There is only one thing that he really loves and that is his bottle. The pig has a cheek to tell you that!" I noticed that his voice was a bit hoarse.

"Do you want some medicine?" I asked him, in an effort to change the subject. "We have some nice green kind. It tastes just like sweets."

"No," he answered. He shook his head in disbelief. "He said what? That he loves me?"

He stared out of the window for a while and then turned around and looked at me. "I must go again," he said. "I just came to fetch the things. Tell Mamsie that I'm all right."

"No!" I shouted. "You can't. The police will come and look for you. Please stay here. Dadda won't hit you—I promise."

My eyes were blinded by a sudden rush of tears and my voice became shaky.

"Please, David!" I begged. "Please!"

"I will come and see you again," David said, taking my clinging hands off his jacket. "I'll come every day. I promise you."

I clung to him, determined not to let go.

"You know your father will kill me," he said, trying to reason with me. "I have a nice place to stay now, with my *broer;* I'm working now too."

He put his hand into his pocket and pulled out some notes. He gave me a five-rand note.

"Here," he said. "Take this money and buy you and Baby something nice to eat. I'll come and see you again tomorrow."

"I'm going with you," I said firmly.

"You can't," he said sharply and stormed out of the house.

He darted through the hole in the fence, but I was after him. I didn't even stop to think that I would be leaving Baby alone. David ran over the field. He was fast, but I followed. I kept my eyes on Stumpy's dirty white body. I was terrified that they would disappear from my sight. I noticed that Stumpy did not run as fast as he did before, or maybe it was because he knew that I was watching him, using him as my compass.

I slipped in the mud and fell flat on my face. I crawled to my feet. My side hurt, as happens when one runs very far, very fast. Determined, I limped on, thinking that as long as I could see Stumpy, I would be all right. David had vanished, probably into the bushes. Where was Stumpy?

I realized that it would be useless to continue. I sat down in the mud to cry. I had lost him again.

"David, David, David! Come home!" I cried.

The next thing I knew, I heard panting close to me—Stumpy's panting!

"Stumpy!" I said, putting my hand out to stroke him. "Look how fat you are. David's *broer* probably feeds you well."

Stumpy looked at me with his mischievous eyes, almost beckoning me on. I could not run anymore, but I managed to trot on behind Stumpy.

"Clever boy!" I said to Stumpy.

The sky was darkening again, threatening rain. We ran for a while longer.

"This place is far," I complained to Stumpy, just about managing to put one foot in front of the other.

Night was falling early, as happens during winter. In the distance I could see a glow. As we approached it, I could see that it was a fire. Stumpy had led me to David.

David's *broer*'s house was also a wood and iron shack, but it was huge. The yard was very big and was not fenced off from the veld. There were about six old cars nearby. Some were wheelless and on concrete blocks, others had flat tires. Apart from one, they all looked like they had come straight from a scrapyard.

The hugest fire lit up the whole yard. Children of all ages chased one another in noisy play. Dogs, cats, and chickens ran among the children. Everyone, animals included, appeared to be doing just as they wished. There was no supervision. The men sat around the big fire, while the women fidgeted about in the house. Every so often a car would drive into the yard and stop, the engine still running. One of the men would get up from the fire and go to the car. He would exchange a few words with the driver and come back to the group around the fire. He would hand the leader some money, and this man would count it and then nod at him. He would then go to the back door and shout "Beer!"

or *"Soetes!"* for cheap sweet wine, or something like that. One of the women would appear and hand him whatever it was that he wanted. He would take this to the driver of the car, who would drive off into the night.

This kind of thing carried on all night. Every time a different man would get up to deal with the driver. David also had his turn. Only the leader remained sitting and only he kept the money. As the night wore on, the men sitting around the fire would get up, one by one, and go into the house. Each would soon be replaced by another man, usually rubbing his eyes. From this I could tell that he had just gotten out of bed. His clothes would be wrinkled, and he would be pulling on a multicolored knitted cap. He might check the fire and, if he thought it necessary, would stack some more logs on it. There was a time when the activity grew less. I noticed that the children had gone to bed and that the animals were sleeping all over the yard—some on the stoop, some around the fire.

I sat squatting at David's feet and rested my head against his knee. He had ignored me all night, but now that his temper was subsiding, he spoke to me.

"Are you tired?" David asked me, feeding me some of his food. It was delicious and had a pungent tang to it. But it set my mouth on fire!

"Let her sleep on one of the beds," David's friend said to him.

Suddenly I recognized him. All along I thought he looked familiar—now I knew. He was the chap that David had fought with at the *vlei!*

"She must go home!" the leader said, looking into the fire. "Do you know how many years you get for child theft? I'm not getting involved. Besides, we don't want the place to be crawling with police."

"We must go home," I said to David, now wide awake.

45

"Dadda and Mamsie will be looking for us. They'll be worried."

"I'll take you home tomorrow," David said. "It's too late now."

"Is it the middle of the night?" I asked David.

"The middle of the night!" David's *broer* scoffed. "The middle of the night? It's almost a new day." He laughed so much that he almost fell into the fire.

I had a sick feeling in the pit of my stomach. My eyes burned. I bit my bottom lip.

I hated him. I hated David's *broer!*

⚜ T W E L V E ⚜

The grass was white with frost when we walked home.

"Carry me," I asked David, so that my numb feet would have some relief.

He bent down so I could climb onto his back. Poor Stumpy stood shivering in the morning air. The cold was visible in a sort of cloud over the veld.

"You mustn't follow me again," David said firmly.

"I want to be with you," I protested.

"I'll bring you things every day," he promised. "But you mustn't tell Mamsie and Dadda and don't give them any of the things that I give you."

I was so tired and worried that I did not argue. I was in trouble.

"Walk a little," David said after a while. "You're getting heavy."

David said that I must go into the house while he waited in the field outside the fence. He wanted me to make sure that it was safe for him to come in. I told him that our parents would have left for work already, but he did not believe me. He wasn't wrong. They were still home.

"Where on earth were you?" Mamsie shouted at me when I entered the house. I could see that she and Dadda had been having words because her eyes were full of tears. Dadda did not look at me, but darted out of the house after David. He must have guessed that David was with me.

"I thought someone had kidnapped you!" Mamsie cried.

"Ag, Mamsie, I was with David," I said softly, ashamed of myself for giving them so much worry.

She questioned me and I told her about the big house and the fire and the strong food.

"Baby was messing in the mud in the dark on her own when your Dadda came home from work. Something terrible could have happened to her, you know! We spent all night looking for you! Your father is very cross with you."

I gathered that much. How could I be so irresponsible as to forget about Baby? I jumped to attention when I heard David and Dadda approaching. Here it comes! Dadda was shouting and swearing. He had hold of David by his clothes and dragged him into the house. He locked the door and threw David down on the ground. "Whose stuff was it?" he demanded from David, keeping his foot on David's chest, ready to kick him if he offered any resistance.

"Please," Mamsie begged Dadda. "Please don't be so hard on him."

"Get up!" Dadda shouted, pulling him to his feet. "Tell me whose things they were. This is your last chance. Who is it?"

David remained silent.

Thwak!

Dadda gave David a backhand smack on his face.

"Are you going to talk?" Dadda shouted.

David stared at him defiantly.

Thwak! Thwak! Thwak!

David's nose was bleeding. It was clear that he would not talk. Dadda's anger was mounting. He got hold of David around the throat.

"I'll force it out of you, then!" Dadda said.

Mamsie was hysterical. "You'll kill him!" she shouted. "You'll kill him! Please leave him! That's enough!"

Baby was hysterical too. I felt so guilty and could take it no longer.

"It's my fault, Dadda," I cried. "I followed him. It's my fault."

48

"Come here, young lady," Dadda said, as if an afterthought had come to him. "Your sister could have been killed."

He gave me a hiding all over my legs with his belt. I was very heartsore and resented the little faces peering through our window.

"Get away from here!" Mamsie shouted at them.

David sat on his bedding pile, looking down at his feet with his hands supporting his head. The blood from his nose dripped onto the floor.

"Pinch your nose with a wet facecloth," Mamsie said. "And keep your head back."

As usual, David did not respond. Mamsie stood holding the facecloth out to him until Dadda grabbed it away from her and threw it onto the table, giving her one of his ugly looks.

"Listen, young man," Dadda said calmly to David. "You pull yourself together and go to school or I'll put you in a place of safety—for your own good. That's a promise. Don't think I don't know where to find you."

David looked at Dadda through defiant eyes.

"You are not my father," he said coldly.

"What?" Dadda roared. "I'll take you to a social worker. She'll work your case for you—and your friends."

David got slowly to his feet. He wiped his face on the wet facecloth and brushed his hair.

"I'll go to school," he said.

❧ T H I R T E E N ❧

I anxiously waited for David's return from school that day and was relieved when I saw him. For a few afternoons he was rather quiet and stayed at home, lying on the bed for most of the afternoon. After a week or so, he was back to his normal self. We were once again going to the *vlei* and watching television through other people's windows. Oupa and Buddy J were our playmates again. More importantly, we were all laughing together again.

"This child is getting too heavy," David complained of Baby, who was sitting on his shoulders, her legs fat and dangling on his chest. They were quite a funny sight because she was far too big for the small David. Poor David was so thin that his legs looked like sticks with knobs where the knees were. These knobs sort of peeped out of his wide shorts' legs, showing up their thinness and knobbiness. David had an impish face and a glint in his eyes, which were large and wide apart. When he was not frowning, he was smiling, showing a row of yellow, rotting teeth and high-cheek dimples. He was not at all ugly, though—instead, you liked him because of his naughty smile. When you looked at David, you would first notice his knees and his grin, but when you looked at Baby, all you saw was the fat tummy that was always showing, cheeks, and slits where there should be eyes.

"Pick that up," Oupa said to Buddy J, pointing to a large wooden box lying at the back of the farm stall in front of the *vlei*.

"That's stealing!" Buddy J protested.

"Ag, you can see that they threw it away," David said, a little irritated.

"Bring that tomato box as well," Oupa said, shoving his stick against a discarded box.

When we reached our hideout under the weeping willow trees, Oupa put Baby in the big box and sat hitting the nails out of the tomato box with a stone. David, Buddy J, and I were playing monkey-monkey. We ran and jumped, grabbing at the low-hanging branches of the willows.

"What are you doing?" Buddy J asked Oupa after a while.

"I'm making a *waentjie* for Fatso," Oupa answered playfully.

"We need wheels," David said thoughtfully, "and a long piece of rope."

"That's easy," Oupa said. "I can get rope, but the wheels will be a problem. Where can we get wheels?"

"I can get some," Buddy J offered excitedly. "In our yard there's an old pram that no one uses. The pram itself is broken, but the wheels are all right."

He told us, laughing, how an uncle of his sat in the pram once and how he fell right through, making a big hole in the bottom.

"But whose pram is it?" David inquired cautiously.

"No one's," Buddy J answered. "We can take the wheels."

"Good!" I shouted. "Baby is going to get a *waentjie!*"

We were so excited that we decided to go home immediately and begin working on the handcart. Baby was cross when we took her out of the box.

"She knows it's hers," Buddy J said, amused.

We sat in the winter sun on the field behind our house while Buddy J went to fetch the broken pram. A number of little busybodies gathered around us.

"Get away!" I shouted, motioning with my hands.

"Leave them," David urged me. "All children are busy-bodies."

"Yes," Oupa added. "We were all like that!"

"I don't think I'm like that!" I protested.

"Take these planks for your fire," Oupa said to David.

"Our dadda doesn't like us to make fires in the house," I said. "He says it's dangerous if you only have one door."

David and Oupa looked at each other in a knowing way.

"Look," I reasoned with them. "If a fire starts at the front of the house, how are you going to get out?"

"What do you people do when it is so cold?" Oupa asked.

"We shiver," David answered.

"Look what happened to 'Sis Mieta and them," I said.

"Yes," David answered. "They all burned to death."

"I remember that," Oupa said. "But they were sleeping when it happened."

"I wonder if they were scared when they woke up and realized what was happening," David said, staring ahead of him.

"Of course they were," Oupa answered. "Wouldn't you be?"

That was a terrible tragedy. People are still talking about it today. What was worse is that a neighbor ran screaming into the flames, trying to rescue her friend and her friend's family, and she died along with them. The following day, the ashes were still smoldering, leaving no evidence of identities.

I was very sad after that, especially when I realized how easy it is to die and how close it could be to any one of us. That was the first time that I thought about the day that I would have to leave my family. It terrified me for quite some time until one night Dadda asked me why I was turning so much in the bed.

I told him all about my fears.

"You die only when your time is up," Dadda explained to me. "And yours is a lifetime away."

I did not quite understand how long a lifetime was, but I felt a bit comforted.

"Do you think it's sore, Dadda?" I asked after a while.

"I don't know," he answered. "I haven't experienced it yet. Now go to sleep!"

❧ F O U R T E E N ❧

The *waentjie* was a great success. I was lucky enough to be taken for rides in it, although it was really for Baby. We took it all over with us and used it to cart our bits of treasure. Everything we saw that could be of some use to us, we piled into the *waentjie* around Baby. Stumpy also made use of the little handcart when he was tired. He simply jumped in and out of it when it suited him. The *waentjie* had to be pushed by either David or Buddy J.

Sometimes they would play that they were on a racetrack. Oupa would then sit on the *waentjie* to steer while David and Buddy J would push as fast as they could. They rode it to pieces, but would find bits of materials with which to mend it. They were talking of making another one if only they could find some good wheels again.

One night the wind was blowing so strongly that it howled most eerily. Buddy J's house had a few loose iron sheets. This made a noisy commotion as the wind blew them from side to side. Dadda, who had had a few drinks after work, was annoyed.

"All they need is a couple of nails," he complained to no one in particular. I was expecting him to get out of bed and knock some nails into the loose iron sheets.

"How do they sleep?" Dadda continued moaning.

Kraaaak, kraaak, karaak, krak-karak, kraak was the rhythm to which I finally fell asleep.

I was dreaming that I was swinging on a long rope swing that was tied to a tall bluegum tree that was sprouting new leaves. I was wearing a pink dress—brand new and clean-smelling—and I had new socks and shoes with buckles and

a pink ribbon in my hair. The sky was the clearest, most soothing blue. Back and forth the swing went, my hair blowing in the breeze that it created. When the swing went backward, I was high above the Kamp. I could look down on everyone and all the activity. When the swing went forward, I was lifted above the *vlei*. It was still and peaceful.

Somehow, a disturbing sound entered my dream. Then I was awake. I was sure that I heard a scratching sound and listened carefully. The iron sheets were still making a racket. Dadda was snoring at his best. Then I heard it again. It sounded like someone scratching on our door. It was a feeble, childlike scratching sound. There it was again, and again, this time accompanied by muffled crying.

I lay on my stomach and lifted my head, supporting it on my elbows. I looked around me in the dark. Mamsie was sleeping, Baby was sleeping, David was . . .

"Shh," he whispered, sitting up. "It's Stumpy!"

"How do you know?" I whispered back.

"I know it's him," David answered. "He must be scared of the wind."

The scratching was louder now, and the muffled whimper became a persistent *Owooo! Owooo! Owooo!*

"I'm going to let him in," David whispered, getting up. "Perhaps he'll be quiet then!"

"Yes," I agreed. "He may wake Dadda and then there'll be trouble."

Stumpy was very happy to be let in. He jumped all over David, licking him on his face. David softly pulled a box out from underneath the bed. He emptied the contents and put his jacket on it. At once Stumpy climbed into the box and settled down. David pushed the box under the bed again. Stumpy was still whimpering.

"What's the matter with him?" I asked David softly.

"He must be cold," David answered.

"There'll be trouble if he wakes Dadda," I reminded him.

"He won't wake up," David said harshly. "He's too drunk."

I laid my head down again and tried to fall asleep, hoping to get back into the same dream. I did fall asleep. It was a deep, dreamless sleep.

I woke up in a fright. David was prodding me on the shoulder.

"What's the matter?" I asked him, rather alarmed.

"Get out of bed," he answered softly. "I want to show you something."

He helped me climb out of the bed and led me to his corner. I could see the box with Stumpy in it. He was sitting up. David lit a match and held it over the box.

"Did you see that?" David asked excitedly as the match burned out.

"I saw Stumpy sitting up in the shoes box," I answered sleepily.

"Look again!" David said, lighting another match.

Stumpy looked very sad—that was all that I could see before the match burned out again.

"Give me the candle," David said.

He held the burning candle over the box, catching the melting wax in his hand.

"What am I supposed to see?" I asked crossly.

"Look!" David said, moving Stumpy slightly. "Do you see now?"

There were creatures in the box under Stumpy.

"It looks like mice or baby rats," I said. "What are they?"

"Puppies!" David answered, beaming in the flickering candlelight.

I still did not understand.

"Where did they come from?" I asked.

"Stumpy is a mother," David explained.

"But Stumpy is a boy dog," I argued. "He has no right to be a mother!"

"We were all wrong," David said matter-of-factly. "He was a she after all."

"What are we going to do with all the puppies?" I asked.

"I don't know," David answered gaily, as if he had not even thought about that yet.

FIFTEEN

"How many are there?" I asked David as I helped him carry the box outside into the dark, windy night. He tore one side of the box off so that Stumpy could come and go as she needed, without too much trouble. He covered the box with a mat and placed an empty box on top of the mat, camouflaging it.

"They should be all right now," David said. "They're safe and warm."

"What is going on?" Mamsie asked when we locked the door.

"Do you know what, Mamsie?" I began excitedly.

"Don't say anything!" David commanded.

"What is it?" Mamsie asked again.

"Nothing, Mamsie," I lied.

I hate telling lies to Mamsie because my face flushes and I feel so guilty for a long time. And then there's the Lord. What about Him? The "sister" from the Wayside Seekers said that He knows and sees all. If I had spilled the beans, David would have been cross with me. I wondered how many puppies there were and whether they had three or four legs. I smiled when I thought of how Stumpy had fooled us into thinking that she was a he. I remembered how we had rescued her. She had grown a lot since then and today she was a mother while everyone besides David and me still thought she was a he.

I looked forward to the following day so that I could play with the puppies. David woke me when he left for school. "Look after the puppies nicely," he said.

"How many are there?" I asked for the fourth time.

He showed me four fingers.

"That's not so many," I said.

"That's enough," David said. "I must go or I'll be late for school."

When Baby heard David say that he must go, she put up a crying protest and crawled after him to the door. He had to give her a piece of bread before she would let go of his leg. She was very naughty because as soon as David was gone, her tears disappeared and she sat with her arms lifted up, indicating that she wanted me to pick her up.

"You're too heavy," I said firmly.

Our two bowls of porridge stood on the table, each covered with a saucer. I got out of bed and poured more sugar—lots more—and condensed milk on my porridge and sat down next to Baby on the floor.

We eat the one bowl first and then the other. It is easier like that because I have to feed Baby. I give her one teaspoonful and take two for myself. She eats so fast that she sits with an open mouth waiting for the next teaspoonful. If I take too long, she grunts like an animal. Sometimes I take long on purpose, just to hear her sounds.

I put a pullover on each of us and then went outside to see the puppies with Baby, as usual, perched on my hip. I slowly uncovered the box.

There sat Stumpy. The puppies were wriggling at her many large breasts. I was quite amazed. I had never noticed that Stumpy had so many large breasts before.

The puppies were so sweet. There were three black ones and a white one. Their coats were shiny and silky, especially the black ones. David's porridge bowl was outside the box. He had probably given his porridge to Stumpy. Stumpy stared at me without even wagging her tail.

"Yes, Stumpy," I said. "To think you were once a boy dog and look at you now!"

I put my hand inside the box so that I could pick one of

the puppies up. Stumpy growled at me, lifting her lip and showing me all her teeth. "I'm their granny," I explained to the suddenly unfriendly dog. "You don't want me to show my sister my grandchildren, hey?" I tried to pacify her, but she growled again. This time the hair on her back was raised.

"You selfish thing," I said. "Just you wait until my brother comes home. I'll tell him all about you. I preferred you when you were a boy. Come, Baby, let's play with the chickens instead."

The chickens were growing fast. They were almost fully grown. When they were small, they were the most lovable creatures and looked like balls of yellow fluff. I would sit and watch them all day. Their mother used to be just like Stumpy, but now she chases them if they come near her. They have grown to be very greedy chickens. I give them three cups of mealies a day, but they gobble them up quickly and then strut about as if they were starving. They are also terribly curious. Whenever anyone passes their *hokkie* they jump forward to see who it is. I sometimes sit outside their *hokkie* and tease them. I poke my finger through the wire. They come and look at it. I hold it very still until they think it is a mealie. Then they all scramble forward to peck at it, but I draw it back quickly, leaving them looking so angry. "Serves you right!" I tell them.

Sometimes I give them grass with their mealies. They enjoy scratching in the grass, eating whatever they can find in it.

"Wait here," I said to Baby, putting her down on the mat from Stumpy's box. "I am going to fetch the mealies."

❧ S I X T E E N ❧

As happens with most new fathers, David brought a crowd of friends with him to see the babies.

"Give us one," his friends begged him.

"I'm keeping them all," David answered proudly and then joked: "You wouldn't have liked your mother to give any of you away, would you?"

"You're only giving me one, hey, Buddy D?" Buddy J asked. "In any case, he won't be leaving his mother because we share the yard!"

All afternoon the yard was full of children David had invited to come and see his "babies." He was so happy. Every so often, he would mix a few teaspoonsful of condensed milk with some warm water and feed this to Stumpy, who had not moved from the box all day. She very gladly lapped the milk mixture from the saucer. The poor thing must have been terribly thirsty. All those visitors must have made her feel nervous, the way she looked around her all the time. To think that when she was a boy dog she was so carefree and now she looked so responsible in such a grown-up way.

It goes without saying that Oupa was there with his good advice.

"You must feed them on mealie meal," he advised.

"To think we all thought you were a boy," Buddy J said, smiling at Stumpy.

"It's Oupa's fault." David laughed. "He's the one who looked and said she was a boy. But it doesn't matter."

David's school friends roared with laughter at the mistaken sex of the dog.

"It's not so easy to see when they're so small," Oupa said seriously.

"Then you should have had another look when he—sorry, she—was older," a clever child joked. David then told his friends that they would have to leave as our parents were due to come home soon.

"Can we come tomorrow?" they all wanted to know.

"I'll tell you tomorrow," David replied.

"I didn't know you had so many friends," I told David when they had all left.

We managed to keep the news from Dadda for nearly two weeks. Then one Saturday Dadda decided to make an early start and clean the fowl *hokkie*. I was helping him, in fear of the worst. I was still thinking of ways to stop him from looking in the corner where the box was when Stumpy decided to jump out of the box with three of her pups hanging onto her breasts.

Dadda was furious. He threw the rake down and straightened up.

"What is going on here?" he shouted. "Are you people mad? What do you think you are going to do with a troop of dogs? There's hardly enough place for the human beings who live here!"

Dadda stormed into the house and dragged Mamsie out. "What is going on here?" he demanded of her. "Do you know about this?"

Mamsie was stammering about not knowing whose puppies they were when Dadda called David.

"What are you going to do with these dogs?" he asked.

"I'm going to sell them," David answered quickly.

"I tell you what," Dadda said, putting his arm on David's shoulder. "I will allow you to keep one of the dogs, but please be sure that it's a male one, and then you clean the fowl *hokkie* for me every weekend. In exchange, I will buy the dog's food."

David narrowed his eyes and jerked himself free of Dadda's arm. He kicked the nappy bucket out of his way and jumped over the broken fence.

"David!" Mamsie shouted after him, but he did not turn around.

"I thought that would be a good way of keeping him off the streets," Dadda was saying, "but he is so stubborn. Just watch how he lands himself into trouble one day, but he mustn't come to me then—no, sir!"

Dadda shook his head and picked up the rake. Mamsie shrugged her shoulders and bent down to pick the nappies up. Baby was already messing in the muck.

"Come." Dadda beckoned to me. I had to scoop the fowls' manure up and throw it into the drum.

"This stuff makes good compost," I said to Dadda in order to test whether he was angry or not.

"Yes," he said.

We worked in silence for a while; then he spoke to me again.

"You are a good girl," he said. "You mustn't change when you get older. That other child—I don't know. I try everything for him, but nothing works!"

"He is already so spoiled," he said after a while.

"Dadda, do you know what?" I started. "I like Stumpy and her babies!"

Before I could say anything further, Dadda explained that it would be too expensive to keep all the dogs.

"Another thing," he said, "every season there will be more dogs and more dogs will have more dogs until there'll be more dogs than people here!"

"But we can sell them," I pleaded. "We can make lots of money!"

"No one has money to buy dogs; they hardly have money for food or anything else!"

"What about the rich people?" I argued.

"Rich people don't buy mongrels!" Dadda sneered and added most disgustedly: "That dog's a mongrel!"

✺ S E V E N T E E N ✺

Dadda was quite fair. He said that we could keep the puppies until they were five weeks old. He said they would then be able to leave their mother. But they would have to go—mother included. Dadda kept his promise that we could keep a male pup, but David did not speak about this. It was difficult for me to imagine life without Stumpy. But I supposed that what Dadda said made sense.

The puppies grew steadily into rough, furry bundles. They were very greedy and guzzled up the food that David put out for them. Poor Stumpy had to growl if she wanted any for herself. She had become very quiet since she was a mother. She now allowed me to pick up the little ones when they ran around in the yard. They were sweet bundles of mischief. I felt sad sometimes when I thought that they would have to go, but then I decided not to let that take away the pleasure that I got from having them for a short while.

Sometimes David, Oupa, and Buddy J would put all the pups into the *waentjie* and take them for a ride to the *vlei.* Stumpy trotted quietly beside the *waentjie,* and I held Baby's hand as she toddled beside me for part of the way because she was too heavy for me to carry for such a far distance.

"You people will have to get rid of the puppies and their mother," Dadda warned, "before I do it for you!"

"I can keep them at my house," Oupa offered when we told him.

"But when Stumpy is supposed to be at your house, you

keep letting her out," David said slowly. "Stumpy is the problem, in fact. He won't let us keep Stumpy."

"It's not my fault that Stumpy gets out," Oupa was saying. "It's the ones who come in last that let him out."

"Her," I corrected him.

"I'll have to make a plan," David said, staring into the distance, as if looking for an answer.

"Dadda is right," I began explaining, but no one was paying any attention to me.

"We can sell her," Buddy J suggested.

"Who will buy a dog with three legs?" Oupa asked.

"Exactly!" said David. "That's why her last owner didn't want her."

"We can take him to the SPCA," Buddy J said thoughtfully. "We can always visit him."

"Her," I said once again. "You keep forgetting!"

"The SPCA will put her to sleep," David said. "They do that with old, sickly, unwanted dogs that they can't find homes for. We can't take her there."

"Do you mean they kill the dogs?" Buddy J asked innocently.

"Of course that's what he means," Oupa said, nudging Buddy J.

Stumpy lay quietly, looking at each one of us in turn. It was almost as if she knew what was going on. Her puppies playfully tugged at Baby's clothes (which as usual showed evidence of her last meal).

Buddy J babbled on about something while Oupa silently watched David, who was sitting with his back to us, throwing stones at the *vlei*. The stones landed painfully short of the water, but he threw steadily on, using all his strength, as if it made all the difference.

"You're sitting too far," Oupa said at last. "Why don't we move nearer?"

David neither replied nor stopped his pointless game.

"Buddy D?" Oupa said carefully.

David placed a hand on either side of him and bowed his head.

"What's the matter, Buddy D?" Buddy J asked. "Don't tell me he's crying over a stupid dog. Yes, he is crying!"

Seeing David cry made me feel very strange. It was a lonely feeling that flooded through me. In a fit of fury, David grabbed hold of Buddy J and pounded a fist into his stomach.

Oupa intervened. "We're brothers, not enemies," he said. "Cut it out now."

"He must leave me alone," David said, tumbling off Buddy J's larger frame.

He lay on his stomach and, burying his face in the sand, allowed himself to sob. Stumpy sniffed at him and wagged her tail feebly, almost as if comforting him.

A lump rose in my throat as I sat down next to him. I stroked his head, but he sobbed on, heaving as the tears flowed freely from him. That was the first time that I had seen my brother cry like that—from the heart.

"Let's go," Oupa said to Buddy J.

They got to their feet and left us alone.

David's sobs stopped after a while. He still lay there with his face buried in the ground. Stumpy looked at me and blinked her eyes seriously.

Eventually David got to his feet and wiped his face on his clothes. He put Baby and the puppies into the *waentjie* and started to pull the car toward the road. I fell into step with him and tried to talk, but all my efforts were met with an angry silence.

"Why don't you put Stumpy in the *waentjie?*" I asked.

"She can walk!" he answered me.

We walked home together in silence—he with his thoughts and I with mine.

It was a disturbing day—no wonder I could not fall asleep that night. I kept thinking . . . thinking . . . !

I had been really scared when David was crying. I suppose it was because he was so alone—there was no one who could help him—and yet he was always there when anyone needed him. He had always been my big, brave brother, and when he showed signs of weakness, I felt afraid. It was a pity that he had hit Buddy J, though. I wondered how he felt about it now. What a problem he had, and answers to problems like this didn't come easily. Perhaps I could speak to Dadda the next day. I thought it would be stupid even to suggest anything to him because he was the sort of person who would not be persuaded to change his mind, but it was something I could do.

"That's a promise, David," I said aloud.

"What did you say?" David asked.

"I didn't know you were still awake," I said, surprised.

After a while he sighed and said: "I'm sure that if Stumpy was your dog, it would have been a different case altogether!"

I did not agree with this but did not say so.

Silence followed, in which we were both aware of the other and of what had been said.

"It's not your fault," he said, just as I was dozing off.

I would speak to Dadda in the morning.

❧ E I G H T E E N ❧

"Have you got no ears?" Dadda shouted at me.

"But Dadda . . ." I stammered.

"No!" he shouted. "And that's the end of it! I want to hear no more. That's final! Understand? Final!"

David looked at me sympathetically. He could see that it was useless arguing with Dadda. A little more arguing and he would say that we could not even keep one of the pups, as he had agreed.

Every evening David would take the dogs over to Oupa's house, but when you looked again, they were all back.

"There's going to be trouble!" Mamsie warned David. David decided that we would have to sell the puppies. We went to stand at the traffic lights—he and I each with two pups under our arms while Stumpy and Baby sat in the *waentjie*. No one would buy!

We went door knocking in the richer area, but we were quickly chased away.

"I will try to lock them up," Oupa offered.

It did not help. When we looked again, they were all back, wagging their tails so hard that their whole back sections swayed from side to side.

Nothing helped, and David was becoming more and more short-tempered. Then it happened!

It was a Saturday morning. Mamsie was out doing an ironing job for a friend of her madam, David was fixing the *waentjie*, and Dadda was feeding his plants. The puppies were playfully chasing one another. They bumped against the nappy bucket, upsetting its contents and sending the bench with Dadda's prized plants flying. There was a huge, muddy mess. The nappies were being dirtied by the black, healthy soil, the puppies were lapping up the dirty water, and most of the best cyclamens were ruined!

"*Sies!*" I shouted at the puppies, trying to maintain order. "Stop that! Don't be dirty!"

"My plants!" Dadda shouted. "The filthy *bliksems!* They mess everywhere . . . ! Do you clean their mess?"

He kicked Stumpy so hard that she went hurtling through the air. She landed with a bump on a pile of rusted, corrugated iron sheets and tumbled to the ground. "*Owooo! Owooo!*" she screamed, struggling to her feet. Dadda gave her another kick. I cringed at the sound of the thud of his shoe hitting her flesh. Stumpy dodged the next kick by darting behind David, her tail pulled tightly between her legs. Dadda was in a frenzy. I feared that he would kill Stumpy as he dashed over to David and aimed his boot at the terrified dog. David jumped to his feet and grabbed a broken brick.

"Leave her!" he shouted through clenched teeth. "Leave her or I'll knock your head broken with this brick. I'm not scared of you. You can only hit women, children, and animals, but you're no man!"

Dadda stood still for a brief second before he realized what David had said. Then he lashed out, knocking David off balance. David's mouth and nose began to bleed. Dadda gave the shivering, frightened Stumpy another kick. It looked as if she was bleeding too, but it could have been David's blood that had fallen on her.

I rushed inside to fetch a wet cloth for David's nose. I wished Mamsie was here—perhaps she would be able to calm Dadda. David was getting to his feet when I returned with the wet cloth. He bent down and picked Stumpy up. He did not seem to see the wet cloth in my outstretched hands, and he walked past me and picked up a jug of water, which he poured over his head. He cleared his throat and spat a blob of blood onto the ground. He gave Dadda a cold, sarcastic look.

"See you," he said to me as he bounded over the broken fence with Stumpy still under his arm.

Dadda stood in the doorway. He unscrewed the top of his wine bottle (which was still in the brown paper packet) and lifted his head as he allowed the burning fluid to flow freely into his throat. His Adam's apple vibrated rhythmically as he guzzled the liquid down. One, two, three, all gone. He flung the bottle into the drum that served as a bin, shattering the glass.

"And you!" he shouted at David through the gap in the fence. "I'm warning you—don't ever put your foot in my house!"

"No, Dadda," I urged him. "Don't say things like that!"

"He'll be back," Dadda said, taking one last look at his shape in the distance. "He'll be back!"

I knew better. I would have to talk to David or he would not come back.

I jumped through the hole in the fence and ran after him.

"David!" I called to him. "David, wait! Dadda didn't mean that," I explained, out of breath. "He didn't really mean what he said. He was angry, that's all."

"I heard him well," David argued, firmly but calmly. "I *heard* him well," he said.

"But he didn't mean it," I begged.

"This time I won't go back at all."

"Please," I begged him.

"No!" he insisted as stubbornly as always.

"Ag, please, man," I pleaded. "Mamsie will be home soon; then everything will be all right."

"All right?" he echoed sarcastically. "Don't make me laugh!"

"In any case, he'll fall asleep soon," I explained. "He's finished a whole bottle already."

He turned around to face me, thrusting the poor Stumpy toward me. "Just look at her!" he said, his eyes brimming with tears. "I can never forgive him—never!"

Stumpy was moving her tongue about as you often do when you have a hair in your mouth. What could I say? We walked on in silence for a long time.

"Where will you go?" I asked eventually.

"I'm not sure," he answered.

I thought he would go to his old friends, where they burn a fire all night, but we were not heading in that direction. My feet were hurting from all the thorns that we were tramping over and I was getting tired. We had been walking for hours.

"Isn't Stumpy heavy?" I asked him after thinking about how to get him to stop for a rest.

"She is heavy," he answered.

"Let's rest for a while," I suggested eventually.

"Let's get over that hill first," he said.

We were walking through thick, white, loose sand. All around us were signs of spring. The mountains were a crisp, delicate blue. The sky was clear and little grasses were sprouting beneath our feet. The air smelled fresh and clean.

"Cape Town must be the most beautiful place in the whole world," I said, as I dragged my weary feet up the hill.

❧NINETEEN❧

We had walked for most of the day and were now crouched beneath some *rooikrans* bushes in a sort of dip between rows of white sand dunes. From the top of each dune we could see the sea, although this meant nothing to David.

I was totally out of breath and my head was throbbing.

Had David not been carrying Stumpy, he would surely have carried me at least part of the way. David laid his jacket on the ground.

"Sit down," he commanded me.

He cradled Stumpy in his arm the way you sometimes see mothers do with their sick babies.

"I'm sorry, Stumpy," he said, stroking her hairy forehead. "You'll feel better tomorrow—you'll see."

"Come, let's go home," I said after a while. "Mamsie will be home and Dadda will be fast asleep."

He did not acknowledge my suggestion.

"I'll carry Stumpy for you," I said. "It's nearly night time."

Silence followed.

"David?" I tried again after a while.

"Hey, didn't I tell you? I'm not going home! I'll sleep here under the bushes. Tomorrow I'll go and look for work at those stables we passed."

"What about Stumpy?" I asked.

"They have dogs there. I'm sure they won't mind having her. It's not everyone who doesn't like dogs, you know."

"What about . . . me?" I stammered.

"You must go home," he said. "Tomorrow—not now, it's too dangerous."

I had noticed how David peered in at the stables, as if he knew someone there. Perhaps he did.

The sky became a red glow as the sun disappeared behind the mountains. That was when Stumpy started getting sick.

"Okay, okay, Stumpy," David said comfortingly to her. "Tomorrow you will be all right."

He carefully placed Stumpy in my lap while he took a branch and covered Stumpy's mess.

"We're going to sleep here," he said. "We must not have flies here."

He gently took the fragile animal from me and sat swaying from side to side, tenderly rocking the dog as if she were a baby.

"Go to sleep," he said to her and started singing a slow popular melody softly to the dog.

The sound of cars in the distance had stopped. All that was left was the mighty roar of the sea, becoming louder and louder, as if approaching us, on this dark night. The sky had clouded over—there was no comforting star to be seen, and we couldn't even see the mountains. There was nothing but black night around us and the rumble of the sea close by. The bushes looked like strange figures in the darkness. It was eerie. I was scared.

"Why don't we move nearer the road?" I asked, clutching at David's arm for the heat of his body and the comfort of his nearness. "At least there are the streetlights."

"We stay here," he said firmly. "No one will find us here."

I tell you, spring or not, it was a cold night. We sat huddled together and shivered.

"I don't think I'll be able to fall asleep," I said. "It's too cold."

"I mustn't fall asleep," David said. "I must look after Stumpy."

"Is she sleeping?" I inquired.

"Yes," he answered softly.

"Aren't there snakes and things here?" I asked later on.

"Maybe," he said. "But don't you know that snakes are more scared of people than we are of them?"

He went on to explain that all animals—even the most dangerous—are more scared of human beings than we are of them. That was the reason they attacked us.

"You must keep dead still," he said. "It is the best thing to do."

"Where did you hear that?" I asked him.

"At school," he said.

My stomach was rumbling. I was sorry that I had wasted my porridge that morning. The thing is that during the week I am so spoiled with all the sugar and condensed milk, that weekends, when I can't have them, I'd rather not have the porridge.

Mamsie and Dadda were surely very worried by now. Mamsie would blame Dadda. I only hoped she realized that he had been drinking and that she should not go on too much with him. He could become very nasty if she provoked him.

"Wine is a devil," she always says afterward.

I would have to coax David into going home. We would probably each be given a good beating, but we had no choice—we would have to go home. We could not live indefinitely in the bushes—we would starve to death. I reached my hand out to touch a branch near me. *Jislaaik!* It was ice cold. I missed the bed—I would not even mind the pungent smell of Dadda's feet in my face. I missed the sounds of the Kamp, the men coming home drunk at this late hour, their women shouting abuse at them for being so inconsiderate, the occasional cry of a child, the dogs barking and howling throughout the night, the cats screeching as they darted over fences and roofs, their eyes blazing in the darkness, the crickets singing beneath the floor . . .

Here was the stillness of death and the mighty noise of the sea.

And the low, sad tone of David's lullaby for Stumpy.

❧ T W E N T Y ❧

The first signs of daybreak woke me. The sun filtered weakly through the bushes. Seagulls flew high above us and called to one another.

Kwaaaa! Kwaaaa! Kwaaaa!

They were white with black beaks and a hint of gray at the ends of their wings. Such kingly birds—very unlike the turtledoves that we were used to.

Kwaaaa! Kwaaaa!

They flew in a group, calling to one another. They were probably discussing why we were there.

David and Stumpy were still fast asleep. I was not going to wake them, as they had probably been awake through most of the night. I had pins and needles in my legs, and my neck hurt. It was probably caused by the uncomfortable way I had slept. My hands were frozen so badly that I couldn't feel them.

I was very glad that the terrible night had ended and looked forward to a new day. I stood up slowly and looked around. There were white sand dunes all around us. I scurried to the top of the nearest dune and could see the sea well. I was mesmerized for a moment by the moving pattern of the waves as they rushed forward, spraying foam all over the beach, and then drew back, only to return again.

A tarred road separated the beach from the area where we had slept. It's amazing what a bit of daylight can do. The sea now seemed friendlier, almost calling me. Its roar was also quieter.

To the right of us, also over a few hills, was another tarred road. That was Prince George Drive, the long road that stretches past the Kamp. I could see a row of terraced houses that went from the corner, where the two roads met, as far as a little petrol station. After that, there were only thick bushes. Later on I would go and knock on one of the houses' doors and ask for a piece of bread and some water. To the left were stretches of sand dunes and thick, bushy growth for as far as I could see. In the distance I recognized two springboks grazing in the dewy morning.

If I had had a piece of cardboard, I could have slid down the sand dunes on my stomach and pretended that the white sand was snow and that I was in Iceland, where, David says, you only see snow—snow houses, even.

I was tempted to shout out loud and hear my voice echo back, but I did not want to disturb David. I decided that it would be a better idea to explore the place a bit and turned round to see if David and Stumpy were still sleeping. As my eyes fell on them, I noticed a wire fence quite close to us. There were rows of strange figures beyond the fence. At once I realized what they were and jumped very quickly over to David.

"David! David!" I shouted, shaking him. "Do you know where we slept? Please wake up, David! We're next to a cemetery!"

David jerked into a sitting position and looked around him.

"What's wrong with you?" he snapped at me irritably.

"We slept near the cemetery," I repeated. "The ghosts must have watched us all night. I'm scared—I want to go home."

"I told you that there's no such thing as ghosts," David said, quite taken aback.

He wrapped Stumpy tightly with his jacket. "I'll have to

get her to the SPCA," he explained. "She's very sick. I can't forgive that pig."

"She's still sleeping," I said.

"Yes—she was vomiting all night long. She must be very tired. I wish I had some water to give her before we left."

I told him about the houses that I had seen, and that I was planning to go there later on. "But I'm not going alone," I said.

"Don't be like that," David begged.

"I'm scared of the ghosts," I argued.

"Don't talk nonsense. I'll walk a little way with you then, okay?"

I agreed and he carefully put Stumpy down, so as not to wake her.

It was early yet. There was not a single car on the road, and the windows of the houses were still full of dew.

"I'll wait here," David said, crouching behind the wall between the houses and the petrol station.

"Come with me," I urged him.

"No—they'll chase me away, but no one will slam the door in the face of a pretty girl like you."

David told me what to say and that I must keep trying until I had succeeded. The occupants of the first house peered at me through the window, but did not answer the door. It was only the fourth door that was opened. A friendly young woman and her husband invited me in.

"Good morning, Madam," I said. "My brother and I spent all night in the bushes. Our dog is very sick and our father chased us away. Do you have some bread for us and some water for our dog?"

"Where is your brother?" the sweet-smelling lady asked.

"He's with our dog," I answered. "We're going to take her to the SPCA."

These people were so generous. They gave me a parcel

of bread, meatballs, bananas, biscuits, and a bottle of water.

"Just bring back the bottle," the man said.

I nodded. "Thank you, Madam. Thank you, sir."

"What a shame," the woman said as I closed the gate. "Such a beautiful child."

◈ T W E N T Y - O N E ◈

David did not keep his word. He was not waiting for me. I had to walk alone along the cemetery fence and over the dunes. I was afraid and ran as fast as my legs would let me. In the distance I saw David comforting Stumpy. He looked so peaceful sitting there like that.

"Did she wake up?" I asked, sitting down next to him. He shook his head.

"Is she not perhaps dead?" I asked.

"Don't be ridiculous!" he snapped. "I told you she's tired—she was awake all night. What did you get?"

I handed him the packet. As we sat eating the food, David pushed pieces of meatball into Stumpy's mouth. She would not open her mouth, so he shoved the food between her teeth. He poured water from the bottle into her mouth, but it ran right out, wetting us both.

I thought it strange that Stumpy did not respond. No matter how sleepy Baby was, if you put anything into her mouth, she would always start munching.

"Are you sure she's not dead?" I ventured again.

"She's tired," David insisted. "She'll come right, I promise you that!"

"Perhaps she's unconscious," I suggested. "Oupa says—"

"Come," David said, rising to his feet. "We must go—we have a long road ahead of us."

"First I have to return the man's bottle," I said.

"Don't be stupid," David said. "We can change it at the shop for something nice."

"But I promised," I argued.

"Come on," David demanded. "We don't have time for that."

We climbed over the barbed-wire fence and took a short-cut through the cemetery.

David carried Stumpy and I carried the glass liter bottle.

"That bottle is worth thirty cents," David explained. "We can buy a few cigarettes for me and a few sweets for you, or bubble gum. You like bubble gum, don't you?"

"I don't like to steal from anyone," I said slowly. "I promised them . . ."

"Why worry?" David argued. "They're so rich—do you think they'll even think of you or the bottle again? I bet there's plenty of bottles in their yard."

"But still," I said. "It's not right! There's a shop," I pointed out when we reached the road.

"No," David said. "Not that shop."

We reached a traffic light and hesitated for a while. The lights changed to red and a *bakkie*—an open-backed van—stopped at the light. David went up to the driver. "Our dog is sick, mister. We are going to the SPCA. Can we ride at the back of the *bakkie?*"

The man gave us a quick look-over, then motioned to David that we should climb onto the back of the *bakkie*. "Quickly," he said. "Before the light changes."

In a flash, David mounted the *bakkie* and helped me on, just as the driver was pulling away. The *bakkie* was transporting building equipment.

David shoved some of the smaller tools into his pockets.

"Don't do that, man," I whispered to him. "He can see you."

"He can't," David argued. "He's looking at the road, not at us."

I peeped into the cab of the *bakkie* to see if the driver could see what David was doing. The man winked and smiled at me, then looked ahead of him again. Riding at the back of a *bakkie* is not very comfortable. You have to hold tightly to the sides, or you fall about as the *bakkie* moves across the road. David did not seem to mind. He shrieked in absolute pleasure.

We rode past the Kamp. That, David thought, was hilarious. The man dropped us opposite the *vlei*. We had to walk up First Avenue before we reached the SPCA, David carrying Stumpy, and I the bottle.

The SPCA was full of people with their sick dogs and cats. David told the receptionist: "My dog is very sick. I think she's unconscious."

The receptionist told us to go straight through to the hospital and directed us to another building.

The vet was a woman wearing rubber rain boots and a dirty white overall. David placed Stumpy down on the stainless steel examining table, which was too high for me to see onto.

"This dog is as stiff as a poker," the vet said. "She's been dead for quite a while already. Was she in an accident?"

She did not wait to hear the answer.

"Take it away," she said to her assistant. "Next!"

David bit on his bottom lip and gathered the dead Stumpy up in his jacket.

"I will bury her myself," he said, and walked out.

He walked so fast that I had to run to keep up with him.

"I told you she was dead," I said, panting. "Didn't I tell you?"

☙ T W E N T Y - T W O ❧

It was Sunday, and there were many people at the *vlei.* We walked as far as the place from which we had watched the last owner of Stumpy trying to drown her. David sat down in the shade and, clutching the dead animal to his chest, sobbed silently.

"Why, Stumpy? How could you do such a thing to me?"

He wiped his tears in the furry neck of the lifeless animal.

This was a private matter between David and Stumpy and I did not want to intrude, but I felt that I had to do something or he would go on forever. I gently put my hand on his shoulder. "I'm really very sorry," I said in an effort to comfort him, but he was beside himself and pulled himself free of my hand.

"Perhaps I can find Buddy J and Oupa," I offered, but David didn't reply.

I thought that I would find David's buddies, who were probably roaming about the *vlei* somewhere. I had never seen David so upset, although I had seen him getting the most severe hidings.

I was sincerely sorry about Stumpy, but she was dead now and there were the other dogs. Dadda said that we could keep a male puppy. David blamed Dadda and surely hated him more than ever now. I am sure that Dadda would not have done such a thing if he was in his right senses. Look how reasonable he was in allowing the puppies to remain with their mother until they were old enough to fend for themselves. It's true what Mamsie says: Wine is the devil.

The smell of meat *braaing* made me feel hungry again, though it was not the *braaied* meat that I wanted, but my mother's Sunday roast chicken and roast potatoes. We would definitely go home later on and be given a hiding and sent to bed without food. That we would have to face. We could not run away forever. Perhaps when they learned about Stumpy's death, all would be forgiven. I didn't know—you could never tell beforehand.

I immediately recognized Oupa's strange way of walking.

"Oupa! Oupa!" I shouted, running in his direction and waving my hands. "Stumpy's dead," I gasped when I caught up with him.

"Where's David?" he asked me.

"Sitting under the trees with Stumpy," I answered.

"But you said the dog is dead," Buddy J said.

I nodded. "She is."

"Let's go," Oupa said, taking charge of the situation.

When we reached David, he was sitting up with Stumpy lying next to him, still wrapped in his jacket. I was relieved that he was not crying anymore.

"Sorry, brother," Oupa said, extending his hand to David, who accepted his condolences like an adult.

"Your mother is looking all over for you," Buddy J reported. "And your father said that if he gets you, he is going to hit you dead!"

Oupa gave Buddy J a look that shut him up. "We must give Stumpy a decent burial," he proposed.

David nodded his agreement. Oupa sat on the ground and proceeded to hit at the ground with a stone. As soon as the soil was loose enough, we all set to scooping it out so that we had a decent hole in which to bury dear Stumpy. David wrapped his jacket tightly around the dog and placed her in the hole.

"Stand up!" Oupa commanded us. "Hold hands!"

We stood in a circle around the open grave, holding hands

and closing our eyes, although I must confess that I peeped a little from one face to the other.

"Lord Jesus," Oupa prayed, "we give you the soul of our dear sister, Stumpy. Look after her well!"

"Amen!" we responded, all together.

Oupa then instructed us each to throw a handful of sand on the dog. David went first.

"Dust to dust, ashes to ashes," he echoed as each one obeyed him.

We then all got down on our knees and pushed the soil back into the hole together. Buddy J and David stamped on the grave so that the soil was level with the surrounding ground, while Oupa took two sticks and bound them together with a piece of scrap wire that he found lying around. David picked some wild arum lilies and placed these neatly on the grave. It looked like a real grave afterward, with the cross at the one end and the lilies in the middle.

The three friends stood about, saying how cruel my father had been and how he will "get his day."

"It's getting dark," I said to David. "We must go home."

He looked at me in disbelief.

"Dadda said we could keep a male puppy," I said.

"Your father gave all the puppies away," Buddy J informed us in his usual boastful manner.

David ignored this bit of information. He bent down, put his hands on my shoulders, and looked into my eyes.

"You go home," he said. "It's the best place for you."

"What about you?" I asked.

"I'll find myself a job with a place to sleep," he answered. "But I'll come and visit you. Remember the last time?"

"Can't I go with you?" I asked, not wanting to lose my brother or wanting to face the music at home on my own.

"No you can't," he argued. "I'll be working and you'll

be in the way. I'll get lots of money and bring you nice things to eat.''

I suspected that David might spend another night in the open veld and I could not face that again.

''Do you promise?'' I asked.

''I promise,'' he said, and we slapped each other's hands as he and Oupa often do when they make an agreement about anything.

David took the empty liter bottle from me.

''You won't need this!'' he said.

❧ T W E N T Y - T H R E E ❧

"Where is David?" Mamsie demanded of me.

"He went to look for work," I answered.

"This time of the night? Now, tell the truth!"

"It is the truth," I answered. "Buddy J brought me home."

"Where were the two of you yesterday? Where did you sleep? What did you eat?" she asked without stopping for answers. "What kind of work? Where?"

"I don't know," I said when she took a breath.

"You had better finish your food and get yourself to bed and be fast asleep when your father comes home. He's looking for you everywhere. Will you be able to find David?"

"I think so, Mamsie," I replied. "Did Dadda really give the puppies away?"

"Yes," Mamsie said with a sigh.

The bed was soft and warm. I must have fallen asleep almost immediately. I dreamed that David, Oupa, Buddy J, Stumpy, and I were running over the hills; then we were playing on the graves among the gravestones. The next thing, one of the graves was opened.

"Come and look here," Buddy J called to me.

David was lying dead in the grave and Stumpy was sitting on his chest, eating a large meatball. Oupa was throwing sand into the grave.

"Dust to dust," we all said.

What an awful nightmare. I woke up feeling very frightened in the dark night. I had goose bumps all over me and thought that Stumpy had come to "spook" me. I opened my eyes and slowly looked around in the dark. My eyes fell on David's neat pile of bedding. Was that Stumpy sitting there? No, it was the shadow of the moon through the window. But I still slipped slowly underneath the blankets, covering my head.

I kept thinking of Stumpy and her motherless children, and of David and how strange it was that he loved a malformed animal so much. She had made him cry, which was something that David had never done before, no matter how close he had come. I hoped that David would not be sleeping in the open again. I hoped that he had at least gone to his friends at the big house where the fire burns all night. Perhaps they would give him a job. I still had the digital watch that David had given me. I hid it under the mattress. There was no danger that Mamsie or Dadda would find it because that side of the mattress was so lumpy they never used it.

Perhaps David would go and ask for work at the stables. Or perhaps he wouldn't as it was because of Stumpy that he wanted to work there. He wanted a home for both of them. Stumpy's life had been short, but not without a purpose. She had brought love to my confused brother.

David, where are you? David, my brother, will I ever see you again? What thoughts do you think when you are alone with your mind? Will we ever walk to the *vlei*, laughing, with you pulling the *waentjie* with the happy, hand-clapping Baby sitting inside it? Please, David, don't forget that you have a sister who loves you.

"What time did Anna come home?" Dadda asked as he climbed into bed.

"Not late," Mamsie replied.

"Did you give her a good hiding?" Dadda asked.

"Yes," Mamsie lied. "And I sent her to bed without food."

"Good," Dadda approved. "Bend the tree while it's young."

"She doesn't know where to find David," Mamsie informed him.

I did not stir and made the effort to breathe as one does when one is sleeping.

"We'll have to do something about that boy," Dadda said. "He can't go on like this—he'll end up in jail. It's the company he keeps, you know!"

"I know," Mamsie replied.

"His friends teach him to do wrong things and who must suffer? You!"

That was not true. Nobody, but nobody, could influence David to do anything that he did not want to do. He was pretty stubborn, our David. How little they knew about him.

"It's that Oupa," Mamsie was saying. "I can't stand him. And look at his brother—they're a lot of *skollies.*"

"I was there too," Dadda said. "They say they know nothing of his whereabouts."

"I think I've lost my son already," Mamsie said. "He wants to be a man. Anna said that he was going to look for a job."

"Rubbish!" Dadda said. "What kind of work can he do?"

"I don't know," Mamsie said after a while, sighing again.

"He'll come home," Dadda said. "Just you watch."

"I don't think so," Mamsie said calmly. "It looks like he wants to be a man now."

There was another spell of silence; then Dadda spoke.

"I was very cross, you know, and I gave him enough time to get rid of those dogs."

"I don't feel like arguing," Mamsie said, turning her back on Dadda. She was lying in the middle for a change. I was surprised to hear Mamsie and Dadda talking so politely to each other. Most times it was just swearing and shouting. What a difference.

I wondered what David would do with all the building tools that he had stolen from the back of the *bakkie*. How could he take things that did not belong to him? That was plain stealing. He must not do that! He would end up in jail. I would have to have a serious talk with him when he came to visit me. He had said that he would!

❧ T W E N T Y - F O U R ❧

Every morning I climbed onto the roof of the fowl *hok-kie,* expecting David's approach. Sometimes I sat there all day and would still be sitting there when Mamsie and Dadda came home from work. They would call me in. The only times I would climb down would be to attend to Baby or do my chores, but I would rush back again. I wanted to run out to meet him when he came. Every day I was disappointed. He did not come!

Longing is like a disease that will not leave you. I was feeling lonely and depressed. No matter that the Kamp bustled with activity and that there were people all around me, I felt so terribly alone. I had lost my zest for living and was bad-tempered with Baby, hitting her for everything that she did that irritated me.

A week passed, two weeks, three. I was beginning to think that I would never see David again. I had lost him forever!

"You must eat your food," Dadda would tease me. "You already look like a shadow and if you won't eat, you'll disappear altogether."

I was becoming unfriendly, aloof, and did not want to do anything or speak to anyone. No amount of coaxing or pampering would comfort me.

"Must I feed you?" Dadda would joke.

"No!" I'd snap at him. "I'm too big to be fed!"

"Then just eat a tiny bit," Mamsie would try.

"I can't," I would plead. "I'm just not hungry."

I lay awake for most of the night, thinking, pining. David, David, David, where are you, David? Do you think of

97

me too? Do you miss me even a little bit? Do you remember how we slept in the bushes that night? Where are you sleeping now, David?

I would lie awake and listen to Dadda's snoring. Sometimes I would sit up and look at him in the dark. Somehow he looked too innocent for me to blame. Was he guilty? If so, how guilty? No, it was not his fault. It was David's own decision.

Some nights when I could not fall asleep for longing, I would resolve that I would go out and find him. I would not stop looking until I found him, and even if he did not want to come home again, I would feel satisfied just to know that he was well. When the morning arrived, I would decide against going out in case that was the day that he wanted to come and visit me. At all costs, I had to be there when he came. I would again climb the wire fence of the fowl *hokkie* and sit in the blazing sun on its corrugated iron roof. I would see the sun rise and see it set, and there would still be no sign of David. Sometimes I would resolve there and then that I would have to go out and look for him, but once again, when the time came, I would decide against it. That just might be the day! Every face I saw I thought was David's until it was close up. Buddy J sometimes came and tried to make conversation, but after a while he would leave, sensing that his company was not welcome.

I wondered whether he still looked the same, whether he still wore other people's cast-off clothes that were too big for him, whether he was still "small for his age," whether he had a square meal every day, or a roof over his head at night. I tried to picture him with his big eyes and his curly brown hair. It was probably bushy and in need of a trim. Dadda used to trim his hair for him. Dadda was not always nasty toward him!

Sometimes, when I could not fall asleep, I would lie

awake thinking. Maybe if Dadda had been his real father . . . if Stumpy had been a male dog . . . if we had not gone to the *vlei* that day . . . if we had taken Stumpy to the SPCA earlier . . . if we had given the puppies away when we were supposed to . . . if David had been born a girl . . .

Too many ifs, questions without answers, why? why? why, David? why?

When I dreamed about him, everything would be so real and natural—Stumpy would be there, and Oupa and Buddy J and David would all be singing and laughing and talking under a friendly sun. The water would be glistening in the *vlei,* the grass would be green and lush, and I would be hopping and skipping along with happiness.

I hated waking after such a dream. Most times I would be so confused and look at David's corner as if my world was a dream and the dream was my world.

Sensing my unhappiness, Dadda invited me to lie in his arms one night. The nearness brought the much-needed tears to my eyes. There was no stopping them! As Dadda stroked my hair, I poured forth all those feelings of hurt, wetting his top, but he held me close and let me cry.

"You must cry," Dadda said. "You'll feel better when it's all over."

"But I want him," I cried. "Please find him for me!"

Dadda assured me that if David did not appear by the weekend, he would go and look for him. As soon as I had stopped crying, Baby started. She was so naughty and cried just because she heard me crying.

"Look what you've done!" Mamsie snapped at me.

"Just put her bottle in her mouth," Dadda snapped back.

It was two days later that I saw a yellow police van driving around the Kamp with a growing following of inquisitive children running after it. Some of the bigger children had jumped onto the bumper and had grabbed hold of the back-door handles. They were enjoying a free ride, their faces a picture of mischief and delight.

The police truck stopped in front of our house. Voices on the two-way radio entertained the children even more, but when the uniformed policeman called to them, they were all too reluctant to go forward. I could see that the back of the truck was empty and was a bit disappointed because what point is there in a police van without a prisoner? Suddenly, everyone was pointing at me.

"Come!" Buddy J called to me. "They are looking for Jantjies."

"There's Jantjies' daughter!" someone shouted.

The tall, sturdy policeman walked into the yard and up to the fowl *hokkie*.

"Hallo," he said in a friendly manner and asked me in Afrikaans whether my mother was at home.

I looked down at my hands and did not answer or change my position. The policeman repeated his question.

"She is alone at home with the baby," Buddy J said to the policeman.

The policeman said in Afrikaans that he had a letter for my mother and would I give it to her please? Someone shouted that I spoke English and added: "They are snobbish!" Laughter roared from the other children.

The policeman went to the van and spoke to his partner, who handed him a piece of paper that he had written on. He came back to me and told me that it was important that I give this letter to my mother as soon as she came home.

"Put it in a safe place," he said and lifted me down from the *hokkie* roof. This the children also found amusing. I ran into the house and put the letter on the table.

When I came out again, the police van was turning to go out of the Kamp. The friendly policeman waved his goodbye to me. I gave him a small smile.

"Fetch the letter; then I'll tell you what it's about," Katrien offered.

I ignored her and climbed up the wire fence of the *hokkie* again.

"I'm not scared of the Law," Buddy J boasted.

❧ T W E N T Y - F I V E ❧

It was quite some time before Mamsie or Dadda came home from work, and then Dadda arrived first. Naturally, I said nothing about the letter to him because the policeman had said that I had to give it to my mother.

Mamsie eventually arrived and immediately struck up a conversation with Dadda.

"I went to see the social worker on Broad Road," she told him. "My merrem told me to go there. They said—"

"Mamsie," I interrupted.

"Keep quiet," she snapped at me. "Your father and I are talking!"

She sat down on the bed and kicked her shoes off. I reached under the bed and got her tatty old slippers out for her. She stood up again, sliding her swollen feet into the slippers. She never stopped talking!

". . . And there were so many people there. You first get a number and then you sit and wait. And I tell you, you wait! If they are not having tea, they'll be back after lunch."

"What did they say?" Dadda asked irritably.

"They said it's a pity that we did not have a photo of him. We must really have some photos taken of the children, you know. There's this place in Wynberg—"

"Mamsie," I tried again. "Mamsie?"

"Didn't you hear what your mother said?" Dadda roared. "We are talking!"

"They say they have hundreds of children like that on their books. Some they find, some they don't, but I know they'll find David. I have a feeling."

She took Baby from Dadda and gave her a big kiss and

tickled her all over her back and stomach. She blew hard on Baby's stomach so that it made a loud sound and set Baby chuckling.

"Mamsie . . . Mamsie . . ." I tried yet again to attract her attention.

"Say what you want to say," Mamsie said, not taking particular notice of me.

"The police were here. They left a letter for you."

"Police?" Dadda roared, widening his eyes. "What did they want? Where's the letter? Why didn't you say anything to us earlier?"

Can you believe that? Why didn't I say anything to them earlier? Grown-ups!

I handed the letter to Mamsie, but Dadda grabbed it from me. "Let me read it!" he said.

The two of them pored over the piece of paper with the bad handwriting.

" 'Please . . . call at . . . the . . . police station' . . . that must be 'regarding your son David,' " Dadda read. "It is definitely something to do with David."

"We'll have to go immediately," Mamsie said, shaking her head. "What has that child done now?"

Dadda carried on about having been home so long and my not saying anything earlier. They decided that they would have something to eat and then they would go to the police station.

"I always said the day would come . . ." Dadda said, chewing on a bone. "You never wanted to believe me!"

I could see that Mamsie was getting cross with him, but she knew better than to answer him.

They locked the door and left Baby and me on the bed. I was too excited to sleep, but of course, could not open the door. This was the first news of David in a long, long time. I was sure that they would bring him home with them. Soon everything would be back to normal. There was a small thought of trouble at the back of my mind, and try as I might, I could not dismiss it. Just perhaps, if he had done anything wrong . . . I hoped not. Why the police then?

It was pitch dark already. They could at least have left the light burning. I did not know how to light the oil lamp—because it was broken and could easily flare up—and did not think it a good time to try. Baby was fast asleep already and I could not settle down. The longer they stayed away, the more restless I became. I was glad that Dadda had gone with Mamsie. David had his pride. He told me that Dadda had chased him away and that he would never come begging. Dadda would have to ask him to come back home. This foolish pride of David's was his undoing. In any case, Dadda would not ask him; he'd demand that he return home. That would be enough for David. That was all that he wanted—to know that he was wanted and that he belonged.

I tried and tried, but I could not find rest. I tried to wake Baby so that I had some company, but when I poked and prodded her, she made angry baby-sounds and turned over to her other side. She kept on sleeping, probably dreaming the same baby-dream.

Eventually I climbed onto the table and peered out of the window. The sky was black and majestic-looking with many twinkling stars glistening like diamonds on rich, black velvet. A fire in the distance lit up the corrugated iron structures around it, showing up the shades of rust. A family of light clouds passed by the moon in a ghostly fashion. And Kamp sounds vibrated all over the Kamp. Music blared, men laughed, children shrieked, and women talked to one another, exchanging bits of news.

As I had started yawning, I went to lie down next to Baby again. Every time I heard someone approaching, I would sit up and strain my ears in an effort to identify the rhythm of the footsteps. I would then lie down again, yawning, but not able to fall asleep.

Kriek, kriek, kriek, the crickets started under the floor. The night was quieting down as most of the residents of the Kamp decided to settle down for a night's rest.

My eyes were becoming heavy, heavy, heavy. But sleep was still teasing me. I lifted my fat, sleeping sister into my arms and sat rocking her to and fro for want of something to do. I did not hear them coming, but was brought to earth with the key turning in the door. Mamsie and Dadda, but no David. I knew that they would not tell me anything, so I pretended to be asleep. I would learn more from them by listening to their conversation.

Mamsie was crying, muffled crying. Dadda was no help to her either. "Stop crying," he said. "Be glad that they have caught him now. He could have grown up to do worse before being caught out. He could become a murderer. How would you like that? Now he still has the chance to learn from his mistakes. He's still young."

"But what would they be doing with so much *dagga?*" Mamsie cried.

"They smoke it," Dadda said, and I almost sensed gloating in his tone. "You don't like me to say anything about that child. How long ago did I tell you that he was smoking? And now? *Dagga!* In all my life . . ."

"They wouldn't even let me see him," Mamsie cried.

Dadda carried on about "bending the tree while it's young."

". . . And you didn't want me to hit him and now he's gone on to *dagga* and you want to cry. . . ."

I felt myself grow older. How was I going to face that? David was in trouble with the police! *Dagga*—marijuana—was at the bottom of the trouble. David, my David—so young.

❧ T W E N T Y - S I X ❧

The roof of the fowl *hokkie* had become a favorite place of mine. I would sit there in a squatting position for hours, just thinking. Sometimes it seemed that there were too many people around me and that I could not concentrate on my thoughts, but from the roof of the *hokkie,* it would be quite easy. After a long thinking session, I felt that I could once again face the world.

It was from the *hokkie* roof that I saw the white Volkswagen Beetle stop in front of our house. A fat, short woman got out of the car and bent over in order to push her seat forward so that her backseat passengers could get out of the car. The children of the Kamp sniggered and pointed at the woman's fat thighs as she bent down.

It was Mamsie getting out of the car from the backseat, and David. It was David!

He was a sorry sight. His clothes were badly torn, and his bony elbows protruded through a dirty green shirt that was so frayed it was hardly recognizable as a shirt. As for the short pants that he wore, if he had not had his hands in what remained of the pockets, they would have fallen down. He looked thinner than ever and his eyes were watery.

David ran into the house with his head bent. The fat lady locked her car and followed Mamsie, who spoke the loudest put-on rubbish I had ever heard.

"Get down from there at once!" she said, pointing a finger at me. "You know I don't want you to sit up there!"

The fat lady smiled at me. She carried a small handbag, a pen, and a folder. Why did Mamsie have to embarrass me in front of her? She was showing off!

Obediently, I climbed down and followed them into the house, dragging Baby behind me. I noticed that all the children were staring into the lady's car, their dirty faces and heads against the windows. I motioned with my head to Buddy J. He immediately went and chased the children away. Mamsie took Baby from me and gave me a smack, showing off, you see!

"That's for being disobedient," she said.

David sat on his pile of bedding in the corner, still looking down. I sat at his feet on the floor. He looked at me and smiled a secret half-smile and winked his eye at me.

I felt like a millionaire and showed him my thumb the way he and Oupa used to show each other their thumbs when he was not allowed to play with Oupa. He winked at me again.

"Give the lady a chair, David," Mamsie said in her new voice. The lady wrote in her folder as she asked questions and Mamsie gave answers.

"What about you, David?" she said afterward. "You haven't told me anything yet."

"He never talks much," Mamsie offered.

"David?" the lady said again.

David sat with his head in his hands, looking down at his dirty feet with a stupid grin on his face.

"Come, David," the lady coaxed. "Tell us how you landed in that trouble."

David started giggling now, but he didn't answer the lady.

"If it was not for this lady, David, you would still be sitting in jail like a common criminal!" Mamsie scolded him.

"What standard are you in at school, David?" the lady tried again.

David shrugged his shoulders, still keeping his head bowed.

"Today's children!" Mamsie said. "In my day . . ."

"Maybe he will speak to us tomorrow," the lady said. "Don't forget that you and your husband must also come. If you can be at my office before eight, it won't take long."

"But I didn't tell my merrem," Mamsie protested.

"I'll give you a letter for her, but you must come—and your husband, too."

Mamsie ranted and raved when the lady had gone. "Shame on you, David!" she shouted. "What were you doing in jail like a criminal? You had better have your story sorted out before your father comes home and you had better ask him to forgive you!"

David raised his brow slightly—just enough to look Mamsie in the eye. "He is not my father!" he spat.

"I can see what is going to happen here tonight," Mamsie said, shaking her head. "You're going to put me in my grave!"

David took the last water from the bucket and poured it into the basin. With a towel wrapped around his lower body, David proceeded to wash himself.

"Now you take the last of the water!" Mamsie moaned.

"I'll fetch more water," I offered.

"No, it's too heavy for you," David said. "I'll do it."

"You must ask your father to cut your hair," Mamsie carried on. "Look what you look like."

David later threw his tatters and rags in the garbage bin.

"Who is that lady?" I asked him as he playfully threw Baby up into the air and caught her.

He bent down and whispered in my ear, "She is a woman who puts her nose into other people's business."

I giggled the way I used to before when he told me something funny.

❧ T W E N T Y - S E V E N ❧

Dadda did not say anything to David when he came home. He was a bit concerned when Mamsie told him that they had to go to the social worker the next morning. He said that he had to wash cars and had not told his employer that he would be late. Mamsie said that her job was just as important.

"Merrem is getting visitors from overseas," she said. "But I have to go."

She explained that the social worker would give her a letter for her employer and that she was sure that the woman would do the same for Dadda if he needed one.

"You just have to open your mouth and ask," she said sarcastically.

One thing about Dadda, he will never come home drunk when there is trouble in the house. He knows he can lose control of himself. That is why he did not tackle David.

As soon as David came back from the social worker, he took Baby and me for a walk to the *vlei*. He went straight to Stumpy's grave. The cross was still there, but the grave had sunk and the arum lilies were reduced to a dried, brown, shriveled mess that crinkled softly when David touched it.

"Yes, Stumpy," David said. "Look where you are lying now!"

"What is Stumpy doing now?" I asked David.

"She's dead," he replied, matter-of-factly. "The worms are eating her."

"Worms?" I repeated in disbelief.

"Yes," he answered me. "Do you remember when we

found that dead cat and it was covered with millions of little white worms?''

I nodded.

"That kind of worms.''

"I wonder if she is also stinking so much now.''

"She could be.''

"Do you think you'll ever get another dog?'' I asked after a while.

"I don't think so,'' he said, looking me in the eye. "No, I don't think so!''

"And if you see someone trying to drown one, will you rescue it?''

"I would rescue it, but I wouldn't keep it.''

"Why not?'' I asked curiously.

"Just because,'' David said.

I so much wanted to ask him about his experiences with the police, about where he had been and how he was involved in the *dagga* business, but I did not want to spoil his cheerful mood. He would probably tell me in his own time—I would just have to be patient.

"We had better see that we are home before *them*,'' David said afterward.

On the way home, we met Oupa on his way to the *vlei*.

"Buddy D!'' he said and they smacked each other's hands the way they did when they played at being grown men. "I was looking all over for you, Brother. I hear you had a hassle with the Law.''

"Yes, Oupa,'' David explained. "I was working with a mailer. The day that they caught us, I had a few parcels on me.''

I listened intently. So, David had been working for a *dagga* peddler and was caught with parcels of *dagga* cigarettes on him.

"How did they catch you, brother?'' Oupa asked.

"My *broer* said that someone must have given us away.

But I tell you, we made good bread—a hundred rand a week.''

"Have they got charges against you?'' Oupa asked like a professional.

"I don't know,'' David replied thoughtfully. "But my *broer* says he thinks I'll get off for first offense. He's still inside.''

"Where are they keeping him?''

"Pollsmoor. There's no bail for him, but he's not worried, hey. He said he already did time for possession, but that they're quite strict as far as dealing goes.''

"What did your father have to say?''

"What can he say?''

"He came to look for you at our house, but I told him that I didn't know where you were. He looked like he didn't believe me.''

"He is like that,'' David said.

"Maybe your *broer* will get a fine,'' Oupa said. "But it'll be a big fine.''

"The boss will pay a fine—no matter how much it is. He is so rich—it's hard to believe that someone can be so rich. You must see all his cars, and I'm telling you—not cheap, local stuff. Everything works with buttons, even the windows—magic, brother.''

"Did you ever meet the boss?'' Oupa asked excitedly.

"No, we don't know who the boss is. My *broer* says it's too dangerous in case anyone wants to get nasty. We operate from the manager's house. He pays us and everything. Every night the boss sends one of his smart cars to fetch the manager. The manager gets in with the money and comes back with more stuff.''

"Who pays you, then, the manager too?''

"Of course,'' David said. "Besides your hundred rand a week, you get free food and a bed as well.''

"What did you do with all your money?" Oupa asked after some silence.

"I buried it in a tin at the back of the manager's house. No one knows it's there."

"You must fetch it before they find it," Oupa said. "That's a lot of bread, Buddy D. How much have you got altogether?"

"Four hundred rand," David said. "Sometimes you get tips from the customers also. I bought me some smart clothes, but they took them away from me in the police cells. I had genuine leather shoes, man."

"That's a lot of bread," Oupa kept repeating. *"Jislaaik!"*

"I was saving to buy a TV set," David said, "and some clothes for my sisters. They must look nice."

"You can make money out of a TV, you know?" Oupa suggested. "You charge twenty cents a person to watch for the night. The people on the opposite side of us do that."

"No," I interrupted. "My dadda doesn't like a lot of people and children in the house."

❧ T W E N T Y - E I G H T ❧

Dadda and Mamsie could not praise the social worker enough. She called at our house every so often to check up on David, who was answering her questions as she wanted them answered. Somehow she discovered that David was not attending school anymore. I don't know how she discovered that because I was sure that Mamsie and Dadda thought he was going to school. Without having said anything, she arrived early one morning to take David to school. No one was as shocked as David to see her!

David left with the social worker, protesting all the time.

"I actually want to go and work," he said in earnest.

He did not stand a chance. "You're far too young," the lady argued.

Dadda came home with a drink in him one evening. He immediately started picking on David.

"You suppose you're some sort of hero!" Dadda shouted at him as he entered the house. "So you sell *dagga* to make some *bliksem* rich!"

David seemed to enjoy Dadda's challenge. He sat in his corner, defiantly staring at Dadda. This made Dadda more angry.

"Other people's decent children are buying your *dagga* and do you know what it's doing to them? It's destroying their minds. Brain damage—that's what you're responsible for!"

"Please leave him now," Mamsie begged Dadda, who pushed her out of the way.

It appeared that David was waiting for Dadda to give him a reason to leave the house. I was afraid of that by the look on his face. He wanted to be able to say that he had been forced.

"I was good to you!" Dadda roared. "Very good to you—I took you as my own child and what thanks do I get?"

"You must sleep, Dadda," I said gently to my father, leading him to sit down on the bed.

"Where did I go wrong?" he wailed and laid his head on the pillow.

"Leave him alone," David said when he realized that Dadda was not going to say the things that he wished to hear from him. "He's drunk."

"Don't worry," Mamsie said. "Everything will work out fine. One of these days we'll be moving from here—then everything will come right."

"Moving?" I asked, alarmed. "Why?"

Mamsie explained that the social worker had recommended that the municipality give us a house as soon as one became available. "A real house made of bricks that has electricity and running water inside . . ." Mamsie said softly.

"And a bathroom!" I added excitedly.

"I still want to see this," David said pessimistically.

"We already have a blue card," Mamsie explained.

"Where will the house be?" I asked.

Mamsie explained that the house could be in any sub-economic municipal area, but since we had this "blue card," it meant that it would be quite soon. Without the blue card, we could wait ten years or more.

Dadda was eventually snoring at his loudest. Mamsie and I struggled to remove his shoes and get him under the blankets. He sometimes does wrong things and says hurtful things, but I cannot love him any less, even though he makes me angry at times. When he snores so contentedly, all is forgiven. I looked at him and smiled. I know the day will come that he will settle down and we will become a happy family.

❧ T W E N T Y - N I N E ❧

The following day Dadda did not go to work, as his head was too sore. It was just as well, because two detectives came to look for David. They were untidily dressed in safari suits and had large potbellies. Perhaps it was their stomachs that made them look untidy because the safari suits on their own were not untidy.

"We want to know who you worked for," one detective, who was holding a folder, demanded.

"I didn't work for anyone," David lied.

"Your partner already told us everything," the other one said. "It won't help you to lie about the issue!"

"You'll only make things harder for yourself," his companion said.

David rose slowly to his feet. He looked confused and so small—a child in comparison with these two brutes who had no manners.

"I don't know what you're talking about," David said, hardly audible.

"Don't you?" the one with the folder said, and gave David a push so that he fell over.

"You don't have to push the boy around," Dadda said.

"He won't listen otherwise," the other detective said. "If he speaks, he'll stand a good chance of getting off."

"Tell them what they want to know, son," Dadda said to David. "It will be to your benefit."

David stared at Dadda, momentarily confused, and then defiance crept into his eyes again.

"He's stubborn," the one detective said. "Let's take him away and make him talk."

"Leave him," Dadda said. "He'll talk. Let me talk to him first."

"Think of the innocent children they are harming," the same detective said.

"Look how they used you," his partner added.

Poor David looked so lost.

"Are you going to talk?" the detectives asked together.

"We don't want to hurt you," one of them said.

David looked at Dadda and then, panicking, said: "I don't know the boss—only the manager." He explained how they operated and directed them to the manager's house.

"What is the manager's name?" the detectives wanted to know.

"They call him Boetie Louw," David said.

"Good!" the one detective said, looking at his partner. "We know the place."

"Is it there where the fire burns all night?" I asked David when the detectives had left.

"Yes," he said with a sigh. "They'll come and look for me if they find out that I told on them. They don't play!"

He drew his forefinger across his neck.

"They'll go to jail if they kill you," I said.

"What will that help?" David asked. "If you are dead, them being in jail won't help you!"

David stayed home all day. He kept peering over the fence as if he were expecting someone. At night he lay awake, staring at the ceiling.

"Are you worried?" I asked him the following day.

"A bit," he replied.

"Do you think you'll be punished?"

"Maybe," he said. "But I think the court will sentence me to be caned. I don't think they'll send me to jail or a reformatory."

"Are you scared?"

"A bit," he admitted.

"What will you do after the case," I asked him, "if you don't go to jail?"

"I'd like to go and work," he said. "I'm tired of school. There are a lot of younger children in my class."

"What kind of work will you do?" I wanted to know.

"Perhaps I'll get myself a job as a laborer on a building site," he answered. "I know they are always looking for laborers."

As the time for the court case neared, the tension mounted. It was as real as the ground under our feet. Mamsie and Dadda, too, were worried. There was a definite change in David's attitude. He had become quiet and spoke politely to Mamsie and Dadda. He even raked out the fowl *hokkie* without being asked to do so.

I noticed how Dadda stared at him at times. It was as if he felt sorry for him.

❧ T H I R T Y ❧

The night before the court case, David sat on the step at the door for hours. He stared up at the stars, as if searching for some sign, some comfort.

It was a beautiful summer evening. The radio announcer reminded listeners that there were only twenty-four more shopping days before Christmas.

"Come to bed, David," Mamsie called as she climbed into bed.

"I'm not tired," David answered her.

"Come, David," Dadda called. "We want to lock up."

David jumped up and locked the door behind him. He rolled out his blankets and lay on top of them, staring at the ceiling with his hands clasped behind his head and his feet crossed. For his sake, I wished the day would come and go quickly, that everything would be over and life would be back to normal. I suddenly felt the desire to be in our own new house. Did it provide the promise of a new life for all of us?

From what Mamsie and Dadda said, they seemed to think that David's chances of being given a warning and being dismissed were good. Still, the tension was too much to bear. As I lay awake in the hot night, I wondered whether David might run away.

The following morning we were all up early. Dadda shaved for the occasion, which was a change because he usually only shaved once a week. Before they left for court, David came and kissed Baby and me. It made me feel so sad because he had not kissed me since Baby was born.

"If I don't come back," he said slowly, "you can have the things in my box."

"Don't talk like that," I said, a lump in my throat. "You'll make me cry."

I stood on an empty drum so that I could see over the fence and watched them disappear into the tall, dry grass.

I wished I could go with them, but Dadda said that I would not be allowed in and that I had to stay with Baby in any case. Buddy J came and sat with me. He was also eager to hear the outcome of the case. Oupa was now selling fruit and vegetables with his brother. He had explained the workings of the law to David. It was his opinion that the case was too serious to be dismissed.

"I don't think Buddy D will go to jail," Buddy J informed me.

He went on to tell me what preparation his family had made for Christmas.

"What are you getting?" he asked.

"I don't know," I said.

As the afternoon wore on and my family did not return, Buddy J suggested that they had gone to do some Christmas shopping.

"Perhaps Mamsie and Dadda have gone back to work," I said.

"What about Buddy D, then?" Buddy J asked. "Where is *he*, then?"

We moved around to the other side of the yard, where there was some shade in the afternoons. Isn't it strange how we follow the shade during summer and the sun during winter?

We noticed that some people were returning from work already. We went to stand on the upturned drum again and looked out over the field. Eventually I saw them approaching and ran out to meet them. When I came close to them,

I realized that David was not with them. I had expected him to be walking behind Mamsie and Dadda.

"I told you," Buddy J was saying at my heel. "They sent him to jail."

"Where's David?" I asked, but got no reply.

"Where's David?" I repeated.

"Where is your sister?" Dadda asked.

"She's sleeping," I answered. "Where is David?"

"We will tell you inside,' Dadda said, looking at Buddy J.

Mamsie sat down on the bed and kicked her shoes off. She looked worn and haggard.

"Where is David, Mamsie?" I asked, handing her her slippers.

She did not answer me. I realized how alike she and David were. He also had that stubborn way of not answering a person when spoken to.

It was Dadda who told me that David had been sent to a "place of safety" in Tulbagh.

"But why?" I asked. "You said—"

"According to the social worker's report, it's for his own good."

"But he's changed," I argued. "Didn't you tell them?"

"He will be there for two to three years," Mamsie said in a dull voice.

♨THIRTY-ONE ♨

"You like boys, hey?" my new friend Susan said as we walked home from school together. "You're big for your boots!"

"It's not that I'm big for my boots," I protested. "It's just that I miss my brother." I added as an afterthought, "He's at a special school far from here."

"See you!" Susan said as we reached our house.

I let myself in with the key that was tied to a piece of string and kept around my neck like a necklace inside my school dress.

The house was stuffy and hot. I filled the bath with cold water and pretended it was a pool. First I opened the windows and switched on the radio for company. The radio announcer said that there were twenty-four shopping days before Christmas. It reminded me that David had been away for a day short of a year. We had moved into our new house at the beginning of spring. It was a three-bedroom house and had a lounge, kitchen, and a bathroom with a huge white bath. It was such a novelty to be able to turn on the tap and pull out the plug afterward. What a change from the weekly procedure in our galvanized iron bath. The house was in Lotus River.

I sometimes wonder how we managed before in that small place in the yard of Buddy J. I often think of him and Oupa and David and sometimes, Stumpy. Our house is not fully finished yet, as Dadda is making most of the furniture himself and buys wood according to his pocket. Baby and I share a bedroom and have Mamsie and Dadda's old bed. They have a brand new bed.

123

We have the most beautiful garden that you have ever seen. It is like a picture out of a book. At the back, we have a vegetable garden. I started school at the beginning of the year but had to change when we moved to Lotus River. I like school.

Dadda uses David's room as a workroom. He was saying the other day that he would have to build a shed in the yard for his tools and things.

"Time flies," he said to Mamsie. "Before you know it, David will be back home again."

We had to sell all the fowls, but Mamsie was saying that Dadda must build another *hokkie* and buy some more fowls. "There will always be an egg when the cupboards are bare," she said.

Baby now goes with Mamsie to work. She comes home much earlier now because her madam has extra help and Mamsie does only the cleaning jobs. Her madam was very good to us. She gave us her electric fridge when she bought a new one.

"It will be so nice to have a TV in the lounge," Mamsie said to Dadda one evening.

I told them about David's money and his desire to buy a TV set with it.

"We can go and fetch his money," I said to Dadda.

"We don't want that money," Dadda said. "We'll get a TV set in good time, but we'll use hard-earned money—not someone else's tears."

I still have the box of David's things. There was nothing useful for me in that box, but I could not throw it away. There were broken blades, cigarette tops with just enough left for one or two puffs, a few cents, bits of screws, and scraps of string.

The other day I received the following letter from him:

Dear Anna,

How are you all? I am fine.

We picked up a cat the other day. It was bleeding and so we took it to the master who said we could keep it. It is a black cat and is quite young still. We put ointment on the cat's bleeding paw and bandaged it up. We are not sure whether it is a female or male, but we have called it Tippy because it has a white patch at the tip of its tail.

I have passed to Standard Four. I am so glad. I am glad that you like school. Maybe you can be a teacher when you grow up.

It will be my birthday next week. Here it is your birthday on the anniversary of the first day you came here.

Tell Mamsie and Dadda that I send my regards and give Baby a big hug for me. She must be growing big now. I wonder if she still remembers me.

Look after yourself and enjoy the holidays.

Love,
David

✒GLOSSARY✎

bakkie	(Afrikaans) light truck or van, with a cabin and open back for conveying goods, animals, or people
bliksem	(Afrikaans for lightning) mild derogatory word used to express anger toward someone
braai	(braaied, braaing) (Afrikaans) barbecue
bredie	(Afrikaans) thick stew
broer	(Afrikaans) brother
dagga	(Afrikaans) marijuana
hokkie	(Afrikaans) makeshift hut; lean-to
jislaaik	(Afrikaans slang) exclamation used to express amazement
lounge	living room
mealies	(from *mielies,* Afrikaans) dried corn
meisie	(Afrikaans) girl
merrem	mispronunciation of "madam"
nappy	diaper
oupa	(Afrikaans) grandfather
petrol	gasoline
pondokkie	(Afrikaans) shanty; hut
pram	baby carriage
rooikrans bushes	(Afrikaans) variety of plant introduced to South Africa from Australia
sies	(Afrikaans slang) exclamation of disgust
siestog	(Afrikaans slang) expression of sympathy or dismay; "Shame"; "Pity"
skollie	(Afrikaans) hooligan; thug
soetes	(Afrikaans slang) sweet wine

standard	reference to school grade in South Africa. Standard four is equivalent to sixth grade in the U.S.
veld	grassland with scattered shrubs or trees
vlei	(Afrikaans) swamp; swampland; small lake or large natural dam
waentjie	(Afrikaans) handcart

ABOUT THE AUTHOR

DIANNE CASE was born in Cape Town, South Africa. She has won both the Adventure Africa Award and the Maskew Miller Longman Young Africa Award for her writing. About her work on this novel she says: ''The character of Anna, the background of the Cape Flats, as well as the poverty and hardship of the Jantjies family are based on recollections of my mother's childhood. I would like this story to make people aware of a very real section of the South African community.''

Ms. Case lives in Lansdowne, Cape Town, with her husband and three daughters.